Marianne

GEORGE SAND
Marianne

PQ2409
m413
1988

Carroll & Graf Publishers, Inc.
New York

Copyright © 1987 by Siân Miles

Published in Great Britain by Methuen London Ltd 1987

First Carroll & Graf edition 1988

Carroll & Graf Publishers, Inc.
260 Fifth Avenue
New York, NY 10001

LIBRARY OF CONGRESS
Library of Congress Cataloging-in-Publication Data

Sand, George, 1804–1876.
  [Marianne. English]
  Marianne / George Sand; edited and translated by Siân Miles.
     p.   cm.
  ISBN 0-88184-415-2
  I. Miles, Siân.   II. Title.
PQ2409.M413   1988
843'.7—dc19   88-7308
                                                               CIP

ISBN: 0-88184-415-2

Manufactured in the United States of America

Contents

Acknowledgements

The introduction is based largely on the following books: George Sand, *Correspondance* (*Textes réunis, classés et annotés par Georgea Lubin*, 20 vols), *Histoire de ma vie*, *Lettres d'un voyageur*, *Questions politiques et sociales* and *Un hiver à Majorque*; C. Cate, *George Sand*; Françine Mallet, *George Sand*; André Maurois, *Lélia ou la vie de George Sand*. A bibliography of the works of George Sand and suggestions for further reading may be found at the end of the book.

I am most grateful for their help and support to M. Jacques Suffel of the Bibliothèque Spoelberch de Lovenjoul at Chantilly, to Elisabeth Tabouis of the Taylorian Institution Library in Oxford, to Peter Larkin of the University of Warwick Library and to the British Academy. I would also like to thank Anne Summers, Marie-Thérèse Allen, Janet Goodfellow, Catherine Hoskyns and Elsbeth Lindner, together with Eleanor and James Partridge, for their suggestions and encouragement and Francis Snyder, as always, for his.

Preface

The name George Sand is that of one of the most renowned
iconoclasts in the world and the *frisson* attached to it is
powerful even today. She was among the most celebrated
and influential figures of the nineteenth century not only in
France but throughout Europe. Coming from a misallied
aristocracy on her father's side and from the proletariat on
her mother's, she belonged to neither class, and despite
strenuous and renewed attempts by a largely male-dominated society to master her, she belonged to no man either.
Revolutionary even by today's standards, George Sand in her
time was a phenomenon. Much admired by Henry James,
Oscar Wilde, Matthew Arnold and the French philosopher
Alain, she was the friend, support or counsellor of an entire
generation of writers and playwrights which included
Turgenev, Dumas *père* and *fils*, Sainte-Beuve, Musset,
Balzac, Vigny and Heinrich Heine; of musicians, most
notably Liszt and Chopin; and of painters, such as
Delacroix. The peroration at her funeral was prepared by
Victor Hugo and one of the most bereaved mourners at that
ceremony was her old and cherished friend Flaubert. Distinguished English literary visitors received by her in Paris,
including Robert Browning and Elizabeth Barrett Browning, kept careful note of her every gesture, and pilgrimages
by ordinary men and women to the small country mansion of
the 'Good Lady of Nohant' continue to this day.

Her name as a writer was more widely known even than
Dickens' in nineteenth-century Europe and her novels were,

as Georges Lubin, the great *sandiste*, has phrased it, 'the Trojan horse in which liberal ideas travelled for the first time into Tzarist Russia'. Documentary literature, pamphlets and articles expressing a subversive or revolutionary ideology were seized by the censor at the Prussian, Russian and Austrian borders but George Sand's novels, which contained similar ideas, were passed as harmless. In his *A Writer's Notebook*, Dostoevsky wrote:

> George Sand's appearance on the literary scene coincided with the first years of my youth. It should be remembered that, in those distant days, novels were the only works allowed into Russia, whilst all the rest, all thought, especially from France was strictly forbidden. What happened? At that time, anything that came into Russia in the form of a novel performed not only the same service to the cause but in perhaps the most dangerous way; for those times at least, for it is certain that those who wished to read Louis Reybaud* were few, whilst George Sand's readers numbered thousands . . .
> The great mass of readers in the 1840s, in our part of the world at least, knew that George Sand was one of the most brilliant, the most indomitable, and the most perfect champions . . .

Her output was prodigious, even by the demanding standards of the period. She wrote nearly sixty novels, twenty-five plays, an autobiography and hundreds of essays, articles and reviews. Yet little of this early feminist pioneer's work is published in English today. Of her entire *oeuvre*, only a few examples – and these from her early romantic period – are produced, primarily in the United States. The reasons for this curious omission might be viewed as threefold.

---

*Louis Reybaud: social economist and writer, best known for his satires on life under the July Monarchy.

First, those works of hers to have 'survived' support a peculiarly Anglo-Saxon sterotype of George Sand, the famous lover. The romantic novels, being very literally sensational, are more easily connected with a flamboyant and extravagant personality. The exotic and the outrageous are more conveniently associated with the stories of George Sand's scandalous liaisons, and the Creole maids, Italian lovers, suicide pacts on desert islands perpetuate the myth of an escapist 'women's writer'. As her work became known in Britain, it was almost always in the context of her own personal history:

> Of the lady herself, though very much has been said and written, we shall say but little here. Few persons have supplied more subject matter of gossip and scandal to the salons and coteries of the Parisians; and few names have achieved a greater notoriety in that world, which to all Frenchmen is *the* world, than that which our authoress has thought proper to adopt. Nevertheless, we doubt whether the readers of these pages would thank us for the reproduction of the *chronique scandaleuse* of those irregularities and eccentricities which have so materially assisted this lady's literary talents in keeping her continually before the eyes of her compatriots. The general statements of a few facts will be sufficient to enable the reader to estimate the tendency of those principles which we shall find developed in her works, as manifested in their influence on her own character. And it is in this point of view chiefly that the private characters of moralists – and all writers, save those on the exact sciences, are more or less moralists – are a legitimate object of interest and inquiry to the public. 'Let us see how the panacea you recommend has answered in your own case', 'How has the moral regimen you advocate affected your own system' are enquiries fairly put to the

proposer of a new code of morals or the supporter of a
new doctrine in the science of ethics.

It is on this ground only that we have been induced to
lay before our readers the following particulars of this
lady's private history – if private that can in any sense be
called, which has long since been as public as thousand-
tongued Parisian gossip, and the hundred-armed monster
whose labour it is daily to record and spread abroad its
cackle, can make it . . .

Foreign Quarterly Review, 1842

The interest excited by her work and the debate which it
instigated were closely associated with her female identity,
and the revolutionary claims she made to a sexual freedom
hitherto enjoyed by men exclusively depended very heavily
upon it. The reflective, pastoral novels of her later period are
less widely read in Britain than those of her Romantic period
whose 'Frenchness' was characterized, in Charlotte Brontë's
words, as 'clever, wicked, sophisticated and immoral'. Even
today, French culture is popularly associated in Britain with
the Romantic tradition.

The second reason for the disappearance of George Sand's
writing is the inbuilt obsolescence of overtly didactic
literature and particularly that whose announced purpose is
the disruption of male-dominated society. Her work was an
expression of the need for women's independence from men
and the unacceptability of her message is undoubtedly one of
the explanations for its neglect after her death.

A third and crucial reason is that because of her sex, there
was one literary and critical criterion by which George Sand
could not be judged. Contemporary writers and critics were
unable to keep in view George Sand the woman *and* George
Sand the writer since those roles were mutually exclusive:
received wisdom was that she had to be an impostor in either

one role or the other. This attitude is not confined exclusively to the nineteenth century. In the introduction to his biography of Sand, André Maurois honours her life and work by conferring upon her the ultimate accolade, maleness: *'un très grand homme'* ('a very great man'). If the Muse (the surrogate mistress or madonna) is exclusively female, and if literature is judged according to the degree of success with which a writer either wins her over or struggles to defeat her, a woman writer who invokes no such presence must automatically be judged not so much inferior as inauthentic. Even Flaubert viewed the act of literary creation as a quasi-sexual activity involving domination on the part of the writer and submission on the part of his subject. He speaks often of his 'bitch of a novel', writing to Maupassant that 'the Muse is the best bitch of all', and when he wrote that 'My poor Muse is dead' he was referring to his mistress, Louise Colet. Flaubert was only one of the many who found it impossible to reconcile the George Sand he knew with the female writer of powerful erotic imagination: 'I find her personally a charming woman. As for her doctrines as expressed in her writings – beware!' he wrote to Ernest Feydeau. The 'doctrines' were based on the principle of reciprocity and the danger lay in the belief that a woman might experience as well as provide the sublime in her physical and emotional life. Though he was one of her greatest allies, even Flaubert, on her death, wrote: 'How much femininity there was in that great man . . .'

The literary establishment of the late twentieth century, like all other establishments, is still predominantly male, and the prevailing ethos within it remains very largely unchanged. Today, both ideologically and linguistically, woman is still the 'other' and her non-normative status is generally viewed as being in the nature of things. Be it ever so slight, and undertaken for the most benign of motives, effort is still required for men to encompass within their natural purview the experience of women. In literature, as elsewhere, women are rarely judged by their peers, or according to the values of their peer group, for whom successful power struggles very often represent Pyrrhic victories.

George Sand's struggle in work was not in order to subjugate or control, but to achieve her own freedom. Her life and her work were in a sense identical and there was in it no division between the private and the professional, as there was none between the personal and the political.

The purpose of this book is to provide an English readership with an example of George Sand's mature writing, which shows another aspect of her work, in the style for which she is equally renowned by her own modern compatriots.

Marianne is an example of the pastoral novels and *bergeries,* such as *François le Champi* and *La Petite Fadette,* which she wrote after reaching her forties. The 'Marianne' of this tale is closer to George Sand's feminine ideal than the Muse of the Republic. In this rustic novella she celebrates the simplicity of everyday country life, emphasizing the importance of superficially trivial incidents which occur in and near the home. Marianne's love of nature reflects the 'moral quality' in George Sand so greatly admired by the mother of Proust, whom he describes in *Remembrance of Things Past* reading Sand's prose, 'which exudes the goodness that my grand-mother taught her to value most highly in life and which I, only many years later, was to teach her not to value most highly in books . . .'

In comparison with her early work, the pastoral *contes* are almost shockingly elegiac. *Marianne* ends with the engage-ment of the two lovers; yet the seemingly uncomplicated nature of their trials is deceptive. The question George Sand was raising – 'Can a woman educate herself without moving from the home?' – and the implication in the story that, if not, she will not marry, was a fundamental challenge to conventional beliefs in the 1870s, as indeed it is in the 1980s.

The quality of the attention paid to small acts of everyday life determines individual philosophy. Nowhere is the integral nature of George Sand's political or ideological concerns and her personal and domestic preoccupations better revealed than in her letters. The edited *Correspondance* of George Sand runs now to twenty volumes and (with ten more years remaining) to over 13,500 letters. Unlike Madame de Sévigné, as she herself remarked, she was not a professional *épistolière*. Save for some letters – such as those concerning her affair with one of the leaders of the Romantic movement, the young aristocrat Alfred de Musset – which were rewritten after the event, they were the spontaneous and personal expressions of a uniquely energetic, and naturally affectionate working woman. In them is reflected the importance she attached to her family and friends and, in minute, sometimes hilarious and always fascinating detail, the daily events of her long and courageous life. For these reasons, it is largely through her letters that I have chosen to introduce this first British edition of George Sand's novella, *Marianne*.

Siân Miles
Leamington Spa, 1987

Introduction

Beginning in the year of the imperial coronation of Napoleon, encompassing the revolutions of 1830 and 1848 and ending five years after the Commune, George Sand's life spanned one of the most turbulent periods in the history of France. Born Aurore Dupin de Franceuil in Paris in 1804, she died in 1876 at her home Nohant in the Berry. Her mother, Sophie-Victoire Delaborde, was the daughter of an innkeeper-cum-birdseller, and her father, Maurice Dupin, was a young army officer, aide-de-camp to Murat, the governor of Paris and brother-in-law to Napoleon. Maurice married much against his mother's wishes and for some time Aurore's grandmother refused to see either his child or *a fortiori* Sophie herself, who already had one other, illegitimate daughter.

The expenses necessary to support Maurice's position absorbed a great deal of the income upon which the young family lived and there was little to spare. Much of her mother's energies were directed towards saving money when Aurore was very young, and to keep the little girl out of mischief, while she herself was busy, Sophie made a kind of playpen out of four chairs. From the safety of this rostrum the future George Sand began her first attempts at story-telling, primarily to secure her mother's attention:

> I used to compose out loud interminably long tales which my mother used to call my novels. I have no recollection of these early efforts but my mother told me about them over and over again long before I ever dreamed of

writing. They were stupefyingly boring, according to her, because of their enormous length and because of the endless digressions I made in the telling of them. This is a bad habit that is still with me, or so I am told. At any rate, I must confess to not having any great awareness of what I am doing. Just as when I was four years old, I have an invincible facility in this kind of creation . . . I could not yet understand how to read fairy stories; printed words written in even the most elementary style did not make much sense to me and it was through the telling of them that I managed to understand what I had been made to read.

Histoire de Ma Vie

Underlying a great deal of George Sand's work is a similar Scheherezade-like purpose, and her literary life of a Thousand and One Nights echoes the themes of survival through diversion and of literature as a means to power.

Her early life was no less fantastic. As a small child she was taken by her mother across the length of France to join Maurice in the Peninsular War and exposed at an early age to a huge variety of contrasts in habitat and surroundings. They were billeted in the palace of the deposed Spanish royal family in Madrid. From its richly hung apartments, where she had been given the Infanta's abandoned toys to play with, Aurore and her mother followed the young cavalry officer in the baggage train, through stinking battlefields, on their way back to France on leave. The young family was travelling together for the first time to Maurice's home, the Château de Nohant, a small manor in the Berry, the most central province of France. From the north of Spain, taking a sloop across the Bay of Biscay and narrowly escaping ship-wreck, they eventually had only six hundred miles further to go. Immediately before this horrendous journey, Aurore's mother had given birth to a son. Food was scarce, disease and infection rife; the circumstances of her pregnancy and the child's first few weeks were far from ideal. The young mother was undernourished and exhausted after the physical hardship, tension and distress she had endured. The relief of arriving safely at Nohant after their considerable trials was marred substantially by the châtelaine's reaction to her daughter-in-law.

Madame Dupin de Franceuil, great-granddaughter of the Maréchal Maurice de Saxe, himself an illegitimate son of the Polish King Friedrich Augustus, was a formidable mother-in-law, devoted to her only son and fiercely jealous of his love for the high-spirited Parisian *modiste* who had ensnared him. The two other members of the household, if not directly of the family, were Hippolyte, the twelve-year-old illegitimate son of Maurice, and Deschartres, manager of Madame Dupin's estate and Maurice's former tutor.

Soon after their arrival, the baby died. The young couple were inconsolable, blaming each other by turns for the death of their son. Eventually, distraught with grief, Sophie asked her husband to disinter the hastily-buried body of the baby. Husband and wife mourned together and, without telling anyone, re-buried the body, but this time under a pear tree and not in the cypress-shaded gloom of the family plot. No one knew the reason for the couple's new joy in gardening together and planting flowers under the pear tree in the week that followed. This story, told to her many years later by her mother, made a great impression on George Sand and an instinct for naturalness and simplicity was to be a characteristic of her life. Indeed her last words, less cryptic in this context were: '*Laissez verdure*' ('Leave green').

Eight days after his son's death, Maurice Dupin, returning home late at night on his horse, was thrown and killed.

The effect of his dramatic and untimely death upon the household at Nohant was incalculably damaging to his little daughter. Thrown together were two women openly hostile to each other; one a witty, sharp, sparrow-like *fille du peuple*, the other a caustic, self-assured and autocratic member of the *ancien régime*. There was naturally a huge gulf between them and, although each was to express strong admiration for the other from time to time, it was a difficult relationship which the passage of time did nothing to improve. Sophie was persuaded to return to Paris to take care of her other daughter, Caroline. In return for appointing Madame Dupin de Franceuil Aurore's guardian and entrusting the child's education to her, Sophie was to receive a pension from the Nohant estate as well as the income from a property in Westphalia inherited by Maurice.

There followed a period in Aurore's life during which she spent most of the time with her grandmother at Nohant, with regular visits to Paris for drawing and dancing lessons, and reciprocal visits to Nohant by Sophie. She was five when this began. Naturally and passionately in need of her mother and missing her dreadfully, she was obliged to restrain and suppress the love she felt towards her for fear of offending her grandmother. George Sand suffered an appalling childhood and learned at an early age to hide her feelings with the utmost skill. At the age of eight, a singularly important incident took place. Sophie, in an attempt to assuage the young Aurore's grief at parting, promised that a time would come when she, Sophie, would be able to borrow some money and open up a hat-shop in Orleans, where Aurore and her half-sister would live happily together with her. Aurore was overjoyed at the prospect. She explained that she would be able to bear the thought of yet another parting provided her mother left with her this promise *in writing*. To avoid an emotional leave-taking, Madame Dupin's maid was told not to allow the girl time for protracted goodbyes; Aurore had time, however, to scribble the following note:

To Madame Maurice Dupin

[Nohant . . . 1812]

I am so miserable not being able to say goodbye to you. You see how sad I am to be without you. Goodbye, think of me and be sure I will not forget you.

your daughter

Put the reply behind the picture of old Dupin.

The following day, her mother was gone and there was no letter behind the picture. The effect of this apparent rejection at such a tender age is not difficult to imagine and its consequences, particularly concerning relations with George Sand's own daughter, were far-reaching. Left increasingly under the tutelage of her grandmother, Aurore was to suffer the quiet agony of divided loyalty for several years to come. Eventually she was sent to Paris to be educated and was allowed to see her mother more frequently; nevertheless, as she put it, by that time 'something inside was broken'.

The establishment her grandmother had chosen for her education was the Couvent des Anglaises, a convent run by English Augustinian nuns near Saint Germain des Près. During the Revolution of 1789 it had been turned into a prison and both Aurore's grandmother and her mother had been incarcerated there, on different occasions and for different reasons. It was a curious choice for an eighteenth-century rationalist like Madame Dupin de Franceuil, weaned on Rousseau and confidently anti-clerical. Aurore was rather hoping her mother would object to her being brought up by nuns. However, no opposition was shown since the Couvent des Anglaises was one of the three best schools for young ladies in Paris. 'It is interesting for us to reflect', wrote one Victorian commentator, J. G. Alger, in *Bentley's Review* (7 August 1859), 'that this great though unequal and too prolific novelist spent three of her most plastic years under English training.'

By this time, however, Aurore was already resigned and submitted easily to the regime. She counted herself one of the lucky girls at the convent since she had 'neither home nor family to miss, whilst others did'. During her time there she underwent a mystical experience, and a kind of religious conversion took place. A Jesuit priest, sensing her difficulties, begged her not to exaggerate accounts of her sins and to return to normal life. She fell constantly between two stools, not knowing which code of behaviour to adopt, or whose advice to rely on. At the beginning of her stay there, believing her grandmother would approve of a stoical attitude, she betrayed no emotion; to her surprise, she was accused in letters from Nohant of being cold-hearted instead. Gradually over the three years she spent at the convent she established a reputation as a popular madcap, and her first theatrical ventures took place here, in the form of written charades.

At the end of her convent career, Aurore returned to Nohant to look after Madame Dupin de Franceuil, who rightly believed she had not long to live. Nohant life was dull and uneventful, relieved only by the visits home on leave from his regiment of Hippolyte, the half-brother of whom she had become extremely fond. Obliged to keep her rapidly deteriorating grandmother company during the nights, Aurore would begin her days, like the heroine of *Marianne*, with vigorous and refreshing rides on her horse through the Berry countryside. Deschartres, who was something of a scholar and an amateur physician, was delighted to instruct her in the study of those subjects not offered at the convent and she soon developed an interest in botany, biology and anatomy. Deschartres had doted on her father and was happy also to teach his new protégée to shoot as well as ride and it was at his suggestion that for these purposes she adopted the more practical costume of a young squire.

She read voraciously: Chauteaubriand, Locke, Condillac, Montesquieu, Bacon and Leibnitz. She also became great friends with a young medical student from the neighbour-hood, Stéphane Ajasson de Grandsagne. Eventually her grandmother died and Sophie reclaimed the right to Aurore's tutelage, turning down the offer of her cousin, René de Villeneuve, of the Château de Chenonceaux, that Aurore come and live with his family. Relations between mother and daughter had over the intervening three years become strained and, after a highly emotional scene, Aurore, now aged seventeen, writes of it to René Vallet de Villeneuve:

> For the first time in my life, I felt angry; the feelings I experienced then were hitherto unknown to me. It was all I could do to limit myself to the following words uttered with the greatest contempt. 'You do not *mind* keeping me with you? When did I ask you to? *Have you not forced me?*' Useless to add any more to this account. You know only too well what I would say. But I must tell you and will never tire of telling you that I shall always remember the kindness you showed me, the sacrifice you would have made for me, the proof of friendship you have shown me and the gratitude I owe you . . .

Throughout her life, René was to be her unquestioning supporter and it was he who first suggested that she might be able to make her own living as a writer.

After the death of her grandmother, Aurore, though technically heiress of Nohant, was still a minor and obliged to heed the dictates of an increasingly capricious Sophie, who had succeeded in alienating most members of her late husband's family. As years passed, Aurore was required to accompany her mother wherever the latter chose and to live totally subservient to her wishes. These obligations included attendance at the house-parties of various friends in the country, including those of the Roëttiers du Plessis who had come to view her almost as their adoptive daughter. It was at their house that she met her future husband, Casimir Dudevant, a cavalry officer like her father. Although within a few months of meeting they were married and she was expecting a child, it soon became a loveless match. Casimir drank heavily, mismanaged the affairs of the Nohant estate and before long began a series of scarcely concealed extramarital affairs. He was brutal in his dealings with Aurore, whom he found both hypersensitive and over-complicated. After several public humiliations, during one of which he struck her, she became depressed and ill. With two of her old friends from the convent, she was persuaded to travel to the Pyrenees in the hope of restoring her health. There she fell hopelessly in love with the elegant and witty Bordeaux lawyer Aurélien de Sèze, to whom are addressed George Sand's earliest literary effusions:

[On the steamer,
11 October 1825]

Can you explain what I am experiencing? Can you tell me
where this delightful calm that I am breathing comes
from? My very thoughts are doing me good! and this
fresh river air is reviving me too. My body and soul are
in a state of well-being which I am incapable of
describing to you but which you understand, since all

that I feel, you feel also, at whatever time of the day or night. Tell me, my brother, how it is we can still be so happy when we have just parted and will not see each other for two months? Ah! I can hear you telling me, 'At last we know each other. We are pure. Our feelings have been raised to perfection. They have acquired a celestial glow. We are proud of each other, we are united for our entire lives, nothing can separate us, we are one!' You are right, my guardian angel. As I watched the earth that bore you fade into the distance, it seemed to me quite clearly that I was only leaving Bordeaux, not my friend! His looks and his thoughts have sailed with me, I carry them around me . . .

The love affair with Aurélien, never consummated, was to remain her only physical relationship with a man which caused no bitterness to either; throughout her life she was to seek, in all rapports with others, the calm which she had experienced only with him. Once she had returned to Nohant, over the next few years the physical symptoms of her unhappiness returned. She suffered from chronic rheumatism, chest and throat infections, coughs and insomnia. As Casimir's drinking and infidelities increased, and as Hippolyte and his mistresses began to join him in his debauches, life at Nohant became intolerable. Aurore's emotional life centred on the rare and chaste occasions when she was able to see Aurélien and the more frequent, less chaste meetings with Stéphane, her first *petit ami*, now installed in the Faculté de Médecine in Paris. She became pregnant in 1828 with her second child, Solange, whose father Stéphane may very well have been.

A new period in Aurore's life was about to begin. She was determined to shake off the constraints of a meaningless marriage, reclaim responsibility for the management of

Nohant and, most importantly of all, find the means of earning sufficient income to bring up her children independently. Although educated, she was trained for no profession, trade or craft, and would be obliged to rely on what native talent and wit she found within her. At Nohant, she had begun to make use of her skill at painting and drawing; but while she was decorating snuffboxes, fans and cigar-cases, Casimir and Hippolyte were very absorbed in political events.

In 1830, Paris had seen the '*trois glorieuses*' ('the three glorious days') of the July Revolution. Disappointment with the reactionary, pro-Catholic and anti-liberal government of Charles X had led to protest within the Chamber of Deputies and its dissolution by the King. Returning an even stronger opposition party, the electorate was shocked when this second Chamber also was dissolved and the electoral law changed through ordinances which included violation of the Charter of 1814 and the abolition of liberty of the Press. Street rioting and fighting had taken place and, in August, the constitutional monarchy of the Orleanist Louis-Philippe was proclaimed. At home, Aurore was discouraged from even discussing the developments taking place. Her frustration grew, changing to shock when she discovered by accident the contents of Casimir's will. It was a declaration of hatred and contempt of her and after reading it she decided once and for all to make the break and leave: 'I told myself that to go on living with a man who feels for his wife neither respect nor confidence is the equivalent of trying to bring the dead to life. I have made my decision and here and now I venture to assert that nothing shall turn me from it.' She planned to go to Paris, remaining there for specific periods before returning to Nohant, until such time as she could send for Solange and eventually also for Maurice, her son. Once again she was obliged, as when she was a child, to live away from those closest to her. She writes to Maurice:

> Won't be long, my little darling, in a fortnight I shall be with you. I can't wait for that time to come. I shall be able to make up for all the thousands of little kisses I have had to miss. Every night I give a kiss to your picture and it sleeps by my bed – not as nice as having you near by. Tell Eugénie to write me a brief list of what you have in the way of jackets and trousers for the summer and what sort of state they are in, so that I can see what needs to be got. Also, will you ask if your little sister needs anything. Goodbye, my little dear. Work well, so that I can see what good progess you have made and love you all the more for it. Give your sister a hug from me, and Léontine, and your uncle and aunt. And you, my dear child, I press close to my heart over and over again. And a big hug to Boucoiran from me. You don't say whether Françoise has had her baby yet or whether everybody is taking proper care of your sister.

Once installed in Paris, and remembering her cousin Réne de Villeneuve's suggestion of a writing career, she sought out as many of her Berrichon contacts as she could find and with one of them, Jules Sandeau, who became her lover, she collaborated in her first literary endeavours. After an initial series of trial-and-error chapters, their first published work was based on a story about two convent girls one of whom wishes to enter the life of the cloister while the other is intent on becoming an opera singer. It was entitled *Rose et Blanche* and appeared under the signature 'J. Sand'. Another Berrichon countryman, Hyacinthe de Latouche, a renowned musicologist and staunch republican whose political sympathies she shared, offered her a job on his journal *Le Figaro*.

The bohemian life upon which she now embarked could not have begun at a more politically and artistically charged time. Paris was in a ferment of political upheaval following the insurrection, and the eminently parodiable utterances and proclamations of Louis Philippe the Citizen-King's government were a journalist's dream. Fearful of renewed public disorder, his government had adopted precautionary measures to prevent a recurrence of the earlier violence. The decrees issued were lampooned devilishly by Aurore who wrote in Latouche's *Figaro* as follows:

> . . . All citizens able to bear arms will parade each day from 7 am to 11 pm . . . During these periods all women, children and old men will perform sentry duty at their own front doors . . . It will be the duty of every householder to ensure that a ditch seven and a half feet wide be dug around his premises . . . that his windows be fitted with bars and that at least 20 muskets be made available for his tenants and servants should the need arise . . . The Government . . . undertakes to unmask no more than twelve conspiracies in any one month . . .
> Each Monday, Wednesday and Friday will be devoted to the foiling of attempts to hold treasonable assemblies, and each Tuesday, Thursday and Saturday to their dispersal.

Her knowledge and love of music earned her the position of arts critic for the most successful satirical daily of the period, but it paid a pittance; she was required also to pay for all her own tickets to the performances she intended to review. Normally, in Parisian theatres, a lady was expected to occupy a seat in one of the boxes but, since this proved prohibitively expensive, Aurore took the advice of a friend who suggested she adopt male dress so as to pass unnoticed in the very much cheaper pit.

The whiff of androgyny already attached to her name

became stronger as she appeared dressed in men's clothes elsewhere also. She paid little attention to it, finding that this style of dress made her, for very necessary practical purposes, enviably unobtrusive. She could go wherever she liked and felt free as a bird. 'Lounging, cigar in mouth, in the *estaminets* of the Quartier Latin and in the courts of its Colleges', as one journal put it, she was able to observe at her leisure and to pass as unnoticed as any young male journalist.

Paris was becoming the musical capital of the world. Giuditta Pasta, the *diva* with whom Pierre in *Marianne* had allegedly been in love, was the mezzo-soprano who took the city by storm in the season of 1831; Paganini was one of the many virtuosi Aurore wrote of in her first attempts at journalism. Liszt was already living there, as well as Rossini and Meyerbeer, and soon Chopin was to be one of the myriad *emigré* musicians to make it their spiritual home. While she earned a poor living by reviewing for the *Figaro*, Aurore was also now writing her own work and in 1832 she published the first of her novels, entitled *Indiana*. For the first time also, she used the name under which she was from then on to be known: George Sand. Having established herself as a writer under the name of Sand, she wished to retain the last name but differentiate herself in some way from her earlier collaboration. There were several different explanations for taking the man's name, George. One was that she recognized that a pseudonym was 'a commodity'; another that it 'preserved anonymity'; and finally, by sheer chance, she happened to be reading Virgil's *Georgics*, whose subject was close to her love of the country: '*George*,' she wrote, 'seemed to me synonymous with *Berrichon*.'

Indiana was received with warm critical acclaim and George Sand's success as its author led to her swift lionization. In it is depicted the plight of a young woman, Indiana, shackled to a husband who regards her more as his property than his companion. She is loved, chastely and in vain, by a nobleman who has already seduced her faithful servant, Noun. The latter, pregnant and driven mad by jealousy, drowns herself. *Indiana* not only painted the ordinary emotional conflict inherent in the drama of marriage but highlighted the suffering of women of both high and low social status. It emphasized the solidarity between them in a world where man's God 'has done everything for yourselves alone, mine has made all species for each other.'

'When beginning to write *Indiana*,' George Sand explained in her introduction to the novel, 'I felt an unaccustomed and strong emotion, unlike anything I had ever experienced in my former efforts at composition; it was more painful than agreeable. I wrote spontaneously, never thinking of the social problem on which I was touching . . . The only feeling I had was a horror of ignorant tyranny.' Gradually, as it became known that the author was a woman, wonder increased, as well as admiration.

The pattern of Sand's future career was set when, on the strength of contracts for the serialization of her next work, as yet unwritten, she was able, to her intense joy, to send for her daughter. Her circle of friends and acquaintances increased considerably and now included the accomplished and impetuous actress Marie Dorval, who was to become a lifelong friend and on whose moral support George Sand heavily depended. Several men in their circle were highly suspicious of the trust and intimacy established between the two women. Alfred de Vigny, Marie Dorval's current lover, was quick to see in it a dangerous and unnatural relationship and tried to forbid Marie from seeing 'this Sappho' as he termed her.

As George Sand's fame spread in Paris, speculation concerning her 'real' emotional and sexual nature grew. One of those tempted to find out for himself was Prosper Mérimée, a well-established writer and author of *Carmen*. The sorry tale of their disastrous sexual encounter did much harm and caused great suffering to George Sand the unnervingly guileless object of his examination. Making it clear that he was not interested in a solely platonic affair, after some preliminary courtship he asked her to sleep with him. She agreed but with more resignation than enthusiasm. To his horror, she refused to behave coquettishly and treated the exercise with irritating matter-of-factness. Whether as a result or not, he was impotent. His fury on leaving her expressed itself in deep contempt for her genuine concern and regret. Confiding in Marie Dorval, she discovered that soon afterwards the story was widely known. For a time she was suicidal – her sexual life was now a talking-point and Mérimée a subject of ridicule; and she was insulted publicly.

Standards of morality, including those of George Sand, have to be set in the context of the rapidly changing society of the times. In France as elsewhere, the period of George Sand's lifetime was one of enormous and turbulent transformation, characterized by a plethora of new, progressive social cults and 'isms'. Positivism, Fourierism, Saint-Simonism and all the many and varied social movements of the period were based on belief in a golden period to come when all previous, corrupt systems of government and social control would be swept aside to make way for an improved order of society. All aspects of morality were questioned and challenged, all manner of substitutes and alternatives suggested and applied to take their place. The principle of mutual interdependence was commonly expressed and experimental societies and communities sprang up throughout the whole of France. The role of women in society was naturally a subject of debate and experimentation within a society already permeated by the spirit of radical reform demanded by the new schools of thought. It was the leader of one of them, Fourier, who first coined the term 'feminism' and the 'feminine question' became one of great importance within each cult. Journals were founded to express the views held on this subject by several groups. Among them, that of the Saint-Simonians, *La Femme Libre*, had to be changed to *La Femme Nouvelle*, because of the 'unfortunate' overtones of the former title.

Within the generally prevailing morality, often women's suffrage was viewed as an expression of clerical reaction. Women had been traditionally regarded as more pious than men and the classic character of the 'dévote' figures in French literature and drama well into the middle of the nineteenth century. To some extent the anticlericalism of the day served to exacerbate mistrust of women. The latter were also in the peculiar position of finding themselves treated as matters of debate and discussion on theoretical and ideological grounds and it was against this position which George Sand reacted. She considered it dangerous to allow oneself to become the object of however well-meaning a group of male ideologues and called for radical reform on a private and individual level.

In leaving her husband and more or less openly taking a succession of lovers, Sand was expressing her reaction to the double standard of the day and not against any one single system of morality. Adultery, for example, was common in both sexes. However, a man could commit adultery with impunity whereas a woman was liable to from three to twenty-one months' imprisonment. If a man found his wife to be committing adultery and killed her, his crime was not murder; if a woman did, it was. Another inflammatory subject was money. In the complicated dotal system of the time, which varied from north to south, marriage contracts under the Napoleonic Code gave the guardianship and administration of a woman's wealth to her husband. Her capital was inalienable but its usufruct the man's.

The serenity and strength much commented upon by those who met George Sand may well have sprung from these early trials in her life. Certainly one of the main characteristics of her private writing is the detachment, courage and humour with which she countered the many and varied expressions of disapproval and contempt for both her work and her person. To a friend she writes:

[Paris, 16 August 1833]

It is both kind and good of you, my friend, to think well of the book I sent you. Not everyone shares your opinion, but you may be sure that I shall consider my detractors ignorant fools and grant wit and reason to others in direct proportion to the warmth of their praise. Besides, since Chateaubriand and Béranger head the list of the latter, you may offer your congratulations with impunity, if I may be so silly as to say so. . . . I am still Aurore of Nohant-Vicq, Saint Chartier, Montgivray, L'Ouroueur, Le Chassin etc* . . . In fact I was very nearly homesick this year but had to stay here because of business commitments and terrible rheumatism which plagued my old bones for three weeks . . .

The thought of her children also bore her up and Sand survived to view the sordid affair with Mérimée with a degree of equanimity. Depressed, however, at the time, and unsure of herself, she was working on another novel, *Lélia*, which when completed caused a storm. In it she suggested that monogamous marriage itself was an abnormal state and that,

*Small villages near to her home town.

in civilized society, women and men were inevitably but unequally deprived of erotic pleasure by its institution. A scandalized *Foreign Quarterly Review* could scarcely contain itself:

> The astonishment created by the sex and individuality of the writer augments an hundred, nay a million-fold as we peruse the subsequent writings of the same highly, but perversely endowed authoress who, in *Lélia*, seems almost ignorant and quite reckless of the difference between right and wrong . . . Decidedly, Madame Dudevant is much more at home in her delineation of matrimonial miseries, than in any other field, that she would well deserve to be called 'the Anti-Matrimonial Novelist' if such a title implied any enviable distinction. The most favourable hypothesis we can frame respecting our disguised lady is, that having been harshly treated by society, and especially unfortunate in the conjugal relation, she has been exasperated into the determined hostility to both, which despite her protestations to the contrary, her publications exhibit, and in the irritation of unhappiness, has lost the sensitive pudicity of her sex.

Lélia is the novel for which George Sand is probably best remembered. 'The subject,' she wrote, 'is none other than the battle between passion extinct and passion reborn, the duel between scepticism and credulity, the ageing and the youthful soul. Lélia herself represents disillusion, suffering, the withering and loss of faith in love, despair. Sténio, her young lover, represents confidence in the future and in love.' It is a metaphysical novel characterized by highly graphic emotional and sexual scenes, which, like all her novels, reflected the contemporary circumstances, characters and events of her own life: Marie Dorval, for example, inspired the pleasure-loving Pulchérie, forming an antidote to Lélia whose own experience has turned her into a creature of marble. Its theme, which was to continue to engage George Sand till her death, was the triumph of love over the 'petrifaction of the heart', 'Love butting its head blindly against all the obstacles of civilization'.

Some English were shocked. 'If the savage represents the degradation of a race and not, as is erroneously supposed, the first element of man, a few George Sands will soon reduce France to a level with the orang-outang . . . Let France look to it, her cup may be fuller than she thinks of the wrath of God . . .'

More important than the satisfaction that this act of feminine assertion was to bring to George Sand, the financial rewards that accrued from *Lélia* were sufficient for her to send now for Maurice and settle him into school in Paris. She had vowed that the life for which she yearned was 'a modest and retiring existence with three friends at most, study during the day and, in the evening, wise and gentle conversation' (*Histoire de ma vie*). A vain hope, given the curiosity her work inspired and the hectic social and literary life into which she was now inevitably drawn. From this time onwards, she was to write on average two novels a year for the remainder of her life.

At a dinner at the *Revue des Deux Mondes*, to which she was now contributing, she met Alfred de Musset, the aristocrat and poet with whom she was to spend a tempestuous period in an already turbulent life. He was a well-known libertine, a sensualist and a dandy, whose sense of humour and style disarmed the initially cautious George Sand. To their mutual surprise, and that of their circle, they found themselves swept off their feet by an intense passion. They spent an ill-fated winter together in Venice where, passion notwithstanding, George Sand's foremost preoccupation, as always, was with continuing to earn her living. Piqued at first by her capacity, not to say need, to fulfill her professional obligations to her publishers, he quarrelled violently with her and then became ill. Matters were further complicated by the intervention, at first medical, then amorous, of Musset's doctor, Pietro Pagello, who fell in love with her. The idyllic Italian dream turned into a nightmare as, on their return to France, she found herself being turned more into the object of Musset's desire than of his love. Disillusioned by his increasingly childish behaviour, and with the final rupture between them imminent, she cut off her hair and sent it to him. It marked a stage in her systematic rejection of a lover whose feelings towards her changed, as they almost always did, from affection or love to possessiveness.

Happier memories of the stay in Venice are recorded in her *Lettres d'un voyageur*. She was captivated by all that surrounded her, including the very subtle and skilful use of language as a tempering device, a buffer against real hurt. 'The 'assurance in writing' on which she had pinned so much hope in her early experiences with her mother was to represent a constant process of intellectual absorption of the shocks she was to experience in her own life:

> Nowhere [outside Venice] is there more talk with less action, more quarrels with fewer fisticuffs. The *barcaroles* have a wonderful talent for insult but only rarely do they come to blows. Two gondolas come round the angle of a wall, on a collision course because of the clumsiness of one gondolier and the inattention of the other. They wait in silence for the inevitable crash; they first see if anything has happened to the boats and if no real damage is done, they start to hurl at each other a few choice words as the boats are disentangled and begin to separate.

As George Sand established a reputation for herself as a writer, and as her confidence in her ability to earn money grew, she became increasingly interested in politics.

Added to the circle of artists whom she regularly saw, her correspondents after 1835 included politicians, social philosophers and lawyers, including Michel de Bourges. The last, an admirer of *Lélia* and of George Sand herself, was the leader of a group of lawyers defending a hundred and twenty-one republicans accused of conspiring to overthrow Louis Philippe the previous year.

The trial became known as the *procès monstre* ('the mammoth trial'). Ten thousand soldiers had been commanded to restore order when silk-workers in Lyon went on strike against a compulsory reduction of wages. The ban on unions introduced in the wake of the strike gradually led to pitched battles in the streets throughout France. Thousands of participants were involved and hundreds of leaders imprisoned. Republicans throughout the land were up in arms. George Sand decided to put her literary talent to direct practical use. Because of the large numbers of accused and the variety of legal argument used in their defence, it was no easy task to draft the comprehensive preliminary statement for the trial which George Sand was instrumental in producing.

Her connection with both political and legal affairs and their leaders, together with her involvement with other men (including by now Michel de Bourges) and the flaunting of her independence, incensed her husband and their domestic battle reached its first peak when she applied for a legal separation against which Casimir appealed. Eventually a temporary settlement was reached whereby George Sand was able to reclaim her ownership of Nohant and was granted sole custody of Solange as well as access to Maurice. The case attracted a good deal of attention as once again George Sand's private life was the subject of gossip and scandal.

In *Lélia*, she had suggested that erotic pleasure depended on casual and temporary encounters and that love, as it was understood in contemporary Western ideology, was in effect a kind of conceit, an intellectual custom or accommodation to the demands made by the social conventions of its civilization. However, she also made it perfectly plain that her own aspirations and beliefs were based on the practice of that conceit and not on the pursuit of eroticism. This was a difficult argument to make in the climate of the times, not least since the proponents of 'free love', and the followers of Saint-Simon in particular, were anxious to co-opt George Sand as a leading figure within their ranks. In a letter replying to a critic who had accused her of wishing to condemn marriage and advocate adultery, she wrote, of her work to date and of her beliefs:

> You say, Monsieur, that the aim of all my books is to inspire hatred of marriage. Allow me to make exceptions of four or five of them including *Lélia* which you list among those arguing against a social institution which as far as I can tell is not once mentioned in it. Of all my efforts, *Lélia* might also serve to rebut the charge you make against me of wishing to set up a 'selfishness of the senses' and institute a 'metaphysics of matter'. Nor indeed, when I was writing it, did *Indiana* seem anything like an apology for adultery. I believe that in this book (in which, if memory serves, no adultery takes place) the *lover*, that *king* of my books, as you so wittily put it, is given a worse role than the husband. And the subject of *Le secrétaire intime*, unless I understand my intentions quite wrongly, is the delights of conjugal fidelity. *André* is neither *against* marriage nor *for* adulterous love. *Simon* has an almost classic fairytale wedding ending and finally,

in *Valentine*, whose dénouement, I admit, is neither novel nor clever, has fate intervening to prevent the adulterous woman from enjoying, through a second marriage, any undeserved happiness. In *Leoni*, marriage is no more the subject of debate than in *Manon Lescaut*. Indeed my literary objective in it was to write a suite to the latter, in which the results of frenzied love for an unworthy subject and the domination of corrupt force over blind weakness are painted in no more glowing colours than they are in the Abbé Prevost's matchless tale. There remains *Jacques*, the only one of my novels, I believe, fortunate enough to have attracted your attention (which, from a man of your seriousness, is assuredly much more than any work of mine deserves) . . . What I do accept as completely true in your judgment is the following: 'The ruin of husbands, or at least their *unpopularity*, such has been the aim of the works of George Sand.' Yes, Monsieur, it is the ruin of *husbands* that would have been my objective, had I the strength of a reformer, but if I have not made myself properly understood it is because I do not possess that strength and because my nature is more poetic than legislative. I hope you will grant me this modest claim.

I always believed novels, like plays, to be studies of morals, in which the *ridiculousness*, the *excesses*, the *prejudice* and the *vice* of the times may be the subject of any number of forms of censure. I have often written 'social laws' in place of the words in italics above and it never occurred to me there was any danger in doing so. Who could suppose it was my intention to alter the laws of the country? Indeed I was much surprised when certain Saint-Simonians, conscientiously philanthropic and laudable seekers after the truth as they are, asked me what I would replace *husbands* with. I naively answered *marriage*, just as I would replace priests with the religion they have done so much to compromise . . .

Again, the main butt of her anger was now, as it always had been, the existence of a double standard governing social judgements over men and women respectively: 'All forms of union will remain intolerable so long as customary law is indulgent towards the errors of the one sex, whilst traditional austerity and salutary rigour subsist to punish and condemn those of the other only.'

The case against Casimir over, for the time being, Sand allowed herself the treat to which she had been looking forward for a considerable time; a holiday in Switzerland with the two children. There, they joined Liszt, his partner Marie d'Agoult, his pupil, the fourteen-year-old 'Puzzi', and his friend 'Major' Pictet. Relief is obvious in all the lines inspired by and recollecting this carefree and hilarious interlude. The party was in high spirits as they found themselves in Chamonix at an hotel full of English visitors who were shocked by their dress, their conversation and their behaviour. Liszt heard himself referred to as 'that fellow' and delightedly adopted the name. Indeed, staying in Switzerland provided them with a private vocabulary that was to serve for some time to come. 'The art of travelling', Sand wrote in *Lettres d'un voyageur*, 'is practically the art of living.' And of the English abroad:

> The islanders of Albion carry with them a particular kind of fluid which I shall call a British fluid, in the middle of which they travel, as insulated from the atmosphere of the places they pass through as a mouse in a bell jar. Their constant impassivity is not the consequence solely of the thousands of precautions they take. It is not the three pairs of breeches worn one on top of the other that keep their bodies perfectly clean and dry through rain and mud and it is not the woolly wigs that keep their stiff, metallic hair impervious to the damp; nor is it the

fact that each of them carries enough pomades and brushes and soaps to clean up an entire regiment of barbarous Breton conscripts; not for that are their beards so beautifully barbered and their nails immaculate. It is because the air around us does not reach them; it is because they eat, walk, drink and sleep within their fluid, exactly as if they were inside a glass cloche twenty feet thick, through which they gaze pityingly at riders with hair ruffled by the wind and walkers with slush on their shoes. As I looked very carefully at the hands, the faces and the general bearing of the fifty or so English men and women gathered every evening in every hotel in Switzerland, I wondered what could be the purpose of so many long, difficult and dangerous pilgrimages abroad. I think I found out, thanks to the Major, whom I questioned very closely on this point. It is this: for an Englishwoman, the real purpose of life is to be able to travel through the highest, stormiest of places with never a hair of her bun out of place. For an Englishman it is to return home after his world tour with never a hole in his shoe, never a speck on his glove. That is why, when they meet in the evenings, in their inns, after their painful excursions, they all, men and women alike, sit in their armour, displaying to each other with smug satisfaction the majestic impermeability of their tourist façade. It is not their person but their wardrobe that travels; the man is the *raison d'être* of the portmanteau, the vehicle of the clothes. I should not be at all surprised to see appear in London one of these days such travellers' tales as: *Rambles with a Hat in the Pontine Marshes, Stiff Collar Souvenirs of Switzerland,* or *Around the World in a Rubber Raincoat.*

On their return to Paris, Maurice became ill. For some time previously, he had been the butt of jokes in school about his mother. The prospect of returning filled him with dread and the fear manifested itself in a form of hypertrophy of the heart whose physical symptoms were extremely alarming. For a time, George Sand and her family moved into apartments quite near the 'Fellows', Liszt, Marie d'Agoult and their circle, which was predominantly Saint-Simonian in its beliefs, particularly concerning the role of the artist in society. In the world of the future envisaged by the progressives of the day, this role was of particular importance. The work of the artist was to be seen as an educational tool in the development of social consciousness. No longer would understanding and appreciation of art be viewed as the prerogative of a small élite. Since literature, painting, music and all the other arts would be valued for their social usefulness, these groups were for the most part opposed to the idea of 'art for art's sake'. Debate concerning the usefulness or the sacred nature of the musician did not much engage Chopin, an occasional though not a regular visitor to the salons of the 'humanitarians', as George Sand, Liszt and their friends were known. A recent exile from Poland, his politics were basically conservative and he entertained none of their high hopes for the transformation of society.

A much more frequent and hugely more influential *habitué* was the most revolutionary and influential religious figure in Europe at the time, the Abbé Lamennais. His heretical and persuasive *Paroles d'un croyant* (*Words of a Believer*), widely translated and disseminated throughout the Continent, had made him one of the most powerful prelates of the day. His argument in that work was that, all men being equal, it was a satanic principle which placed some in positions of power and domination over others. The time was fast approaching, he claimed, when the wealth and privilege that accompanied hereditary monarchies in Europe would be destroyed with the advent of universal suffrage. It was for his journal that George Sand agreed to write a series of contributions, in the forms of letters of advice to a young woman in her mid-twenties. However, Lamennais' radicalism did not reach as deeply as Sand's whose argument, in the *Lettres à Marcie*, centred upon the 'feminist question', which the abbé preferred not to discuss.

Contemporary with George Sand were other women writers and activists with whom she chose not to associate herself. Their views varied widely. Those of Jeanne Deroin, a contributor to the journal, *Voix des Femmes*, were based on belief in the maternal instinct; Flora Tristan, the writer and traveller shot in the street by a jealous husband, was a prominent Saint-Simonian; Pauline Roland, member of the Club de la rue de Taranne, was another of whom George Sand wrote that she had not the honour of her acquaintance. Her feminism differed from theirs in that she was unwilling for women to be co-opted – unprepared and uneducated – into any already established political institution. If this were to happen, she believed that women, in emulating men, would lose the particular perceptions which led them, outside the political arena, to hold in contempt 'the sword and the helmet'. Above everything, including women's suffrage, she placed the necessity for women's education.

George Sand's great-grandmother had collaborated with her husband on a work entitled *Sur les Mérites des Femmes*, to which Rousseau himself had contributed. Her grandmother had inculcated in Aurore certain basic beliefs in the equality of women; yet from the outset of her marriage she was to realize how unfavourably they were treated by society, and she endured for some time a feeling of humiliation and revulsion for the alleged moral inferiority of women as portrayed in the Bible and in philosophical works. All the weaknesses attributed by men to women were, she believed the results of poor or insufficient education; the main source of men's power over women lay in keeping the latter ignorant, with or without the vote.

Lammenais' radicalism differed from Sand's in that the universal fraternity to which he looked forward was confined for the most part to men; sorority was another matter. Although her covering letter accompanying the *Lettres à Marcie* is respectful, its purpose is to alert him to the possibility of wide divergence in their basic tenets:

To Lammenais

[Poste restante – La Châtre
28 February 1837]

Dear and excellent friend,

You have drawn me, unknowingly, into deeper waters than I had anticipated. When I began the *Lettres à Marcie* I promised to write on lighter topics than those to which I find myself drawn by my own poor thoughts today. This frightens me, since in the short time I have had the pleasure of listening to you, and with all the respect and veneration I bear towards you, it has never occurred to me to ask how *you yourself had resolved in your own mind* the questions which preoccupy me today. That is to say, I have no idea whether amidst all the religious and political issues which engage you intellectually, you have considered the present situation of women. The most curious part of all this is that, although I have spent the best part of my writing life on this subject, I have very few principles to rely on, and no succinct summary of an argument; indeed, my conclusions come from a source unknown to me and outside myself, so to speak. I do not know whether I am right or wrong; the certainty I possess is incontrovertible yet whether it be the voice of truth or that of impudent pride I do not know.

Having begun, however, I would like to extend the scope of the *Lettres à Marcie* to include all questions relating to women. I should like to address the problems of duty, marriage, maternity and so forth, but it is possible that here and there I shall be carried away by my own natural enthusiasm beyond the bounds you would permit, if consulted. But do I have time to ask for your guidance on every page? And have you the time to fill all the gaps of my ignorance? No. The series is already under way, I have a thousand other things to think about and when I have an hour or so of an evening to work upon *Marcie*, what I must do is not seek further in my own mind, but produce its fruits.

And after all, perhaps I am not capable of any deeper thought than at present, about any subject. Indeed, every time (I should say the few times) I have had a good idea, it has always come from out of the blue, when I least expected it. So what do we do? Should I follow my instinct or shall I ask you to cast your eye over whatever bad parts I may send to the journal? The latter method has considerable disadvantages; work corrected by another never has the desired unity. It becomes disjointed, loses its logical wholeness. Often repair to some corner of a wall brings down a whole house that would otherwise remain intact.

I think that in order to avoid these pitfalls we should agree on two things – that I here and now outline to you the general areas of possible divergence between us which come into my mind and beyond that, you give me leave to write quite freely without bothering too much if I make some small mistake in the detail.

I am not sure how far fashionable society would hold you responsible and besides I think you care little about the opinion of fashionable society. However, I feel so much affection for you, and entrust myself so entirely to your guidance that even if I knew myself not to be wrong, I should give in, for the sake of your precious handshake.

I should possibly take the most liberty in claiming the right to divorce in marriage. I can see no other remedy for the bitter injustice, the endless misery, and uncontrollable passion which can destroy the union of the sexes; I can see no escape from this except through freedom to break one marital union and form another. I should not recommend it to be undertaken lightly or for reasons any less serious than those which hold now in the case of legal separation. However, (although I personally would prefer to spend the rest of my life in a cell than to remarry), I know there exist some affections which are so strong and so powerful that nothing in our old civil or common law can curb them. Undoubtedly, these affections become ever stronger and more valuable as human intelligence grows ever more refined. It is equally true that, in the past, they have been uncontrollable and that the social order suffered in consequence. The law has been powerless against this social disorder whenever engendered by vice or corruption. But powerful souls, persons of great character, hearts full of faith and goodness have been dominated by passions that seem to have come from heaven itself. How does one account for this? And how can one write about women without addressing this question which is of prime importance to them and which they place above all others? Believe me, I know more about this than you do. A disciple may say only once the words: Master – in this domain, there are many paths which you have never followed, there are abysses into which I have looked while your eyes were fixed on heaven. You have lived with the angels, I with men and women; I know how much one can suffer, and sin, and how much need there is of a guideline to allow people to act decently.

And trust me, no one would search more assiduously, with more respect for virtue, or less selfishly, for I should never wish to hide the faults of my own past; in maturity I can look back with equanimity on the great storms which fade and die on the distant horizon of my early life.

Send me a word in reply. If you forbid me to go any further in this, I shall end the *Lettres à Marcie* here, and write on anything else that you might prefer, for I can be silent on many points and do not feel it incumbent upon me to reform the world.

Goodbye, dear friend and father. No one loves and respects you more than I.

George

Though she did not feel it incumbent upon her to reform the world, Sand did feel it necessary, in the event, to terminate her collaboration with Lammenais, turning her attentions back to her publishers who were clamouring for her next work. There was constant tension between her need to produce and the demands of the children, and when they moved back to Nohant the company of the 'Fellows' did much to bridge the gap between the two necessities. Liszt was excellent company, quick-witted enough to be nicknamed 'the cretin', sensitive enough to take heed of the subtle shift of emotion between each member of the unorthodox family and energetic enough to keep the lines of communication as open as possible between them. Maurice's health was not quite as much of a problem as before, but Solange, as she grew older, gave considerable cause for concern; relations between mother and daughter were often very strained.

Casimir, irked by the refusal of a wife he wrongly believed was rolling in royalties to lend him money, began using both children as pawns in a game designed to unnerve their mother; this included kidnapping. 1837 was a depressing year for George Sand, fraught with emotional and financial problems and continuing worry over her own health, Maurice's and that of her circle. At the beginning of 1838, Liszt (and Marie d'Agoult, who had begun by now to resent her lover's interest in George Sand and her family) had returned to Paris. Sand wrote to them there, using the old in-jokes and apologizing in advance for her latest literary efforts.

To Franz Liszt and to Marie d'Agoult

[Nohant, 2 Jan 1838]

Good-night, dear and charming princess. Good-day, Cretin de Valais. Don't forget your Piffoëls who places at your feet her heart, her cigar and the remains of her scarlet dressing gown. Piffoëls will possibly go to Paris at the end of January. Especially if, as the papers are saying, Berlioz' *Mass* is to be played again. Piffoëls will very warmly shake the hands of *Sopin*, for Cretin's sake and also because *Sopin is very nize*. Piffoëls beseeches Fellows not to read *La Dernière Aldini* but to read next production which is much better and not yet finished.

Piffoëls holds you tight in her arms and asks you to give her any love you have left over from each other.*

While in Paris she wrote, as usual, at least once daily to the children, reassuring them she would return as soon as possible, that Mallefille, their current tutor, would explain the situation to them and Charpentier, the artist, continue to paint their portraits.

*Cretin de Valais: Liszt. Piffoëls: George Sand – a pun on the French slang for 'large nose' ('*pif*'). Sopin: Chopin.

To Maurice and Solange Dudevant

[Paris, 30? April 1825]

Good-night, my angels, my kittens, my little darlings, my
Piffoëls. It's sweet of you, really sweet to write to me
every day. It makes me very happy to get news of you
when I wake up. I need it because all night long I dream
that I have lost you and that I'm looking for you.
Mallefille will tell you why I can't come back yet and be
with you. It makes me even more unhappy than you two
are but it's because of you and *for you* that I will bear it.
Maurice knows why and will tell Solange. Good-night,
my darlings and love the old girl who loves you more
than words can say.

Shake Charpentier's hand for me. I'll try and leave on
Saturday, or at the latest Sunday: perhaps I'll be able to
bring Puzzi with me to see you.

Much as she suffered from the separations from her children,
their peculiar fate was to have for a mother a woman who was
in great demand elsewhere and who needed, and indeed
thrived on stimulus. There can be no doubt that George Sand
was wonderful company. The testimony of countless con-
temporaries – including Delacroix, the painter and later
Turgenev – bears witness also to the particular beauty of her
physical appearance, bearing and demeanour. All speak of
her extraordinary stillness and calm. Comparing her serenity
to that of the Moon, Heine speaks of the 'velvet-soft, dark
unfathomable eyes'. Her remarkably good-natured smile
impressed Elizabeth Barrett Browning: 'Her voice is low and
rapid', she wrote, 'without emphasis or variety of modula-
tion. Except one brilliant smile, she was grave.' The same
gravity and her absorption in others were what struck the
Goncourt brothers when they too were to meet her and
wonder at 'the marvellous delicacy of the small hands'. She

was attractive to both men and women; Hortense Allart, another writer and lifelong friend and admirer, was to comment that if she were a man she would be mad on her. One of her great strengths was that of being an excellent listener. Once she herself began to speak, and once she was in the company of those whom she knew well, she was, said Allart, 'irresistible'. Musset, who loved many, called her '*la femme la plus femme*' ('the most womanly woman') he had ever known.

Now, at thirty-four, she was in her prime and it was in this year, 1838, that the romance between her and the younger Chopin burgeoned into a love-affair. Sand continued her rigorous routine of retiring to work at midnight and continuing till eight or nine in the morning. But unlike Musset and other lovers, Chopin resented neither her régime nor her productivity. Indeed, his presence both increased and enhanced it. When Buloz, the publisher, considered bringing out a twenty-volume edition of her *Complete Works* she decided to use part of the advance to carry out the suggestion that Maurice would benefit from a winter in the sun. Solange was to come, as well as Chopin himself whose health was also a cause of grave concern to his family and friends. Like George Sand's, his labour too was, as it were, mortaged since he had promised Pleyel, the music publisher, a series of twenty-four preludes, one for each major and one for each minor key. Pleyel was to deliver a piano to their chosen destination, Mallorca.

There, after enormous difficulties, they settled in a semi-deserted monastery, the Charterhouse of Valldemosa. Initially, they were able to enjoy the warmth and seclusion of their new exotic home. But the weather did not remain fine, there were fearful problems concerning heating and cooking and eventually Chopin's already weak chest was affected by the advent of wintry winds. The weather worsened, complications increased and the obstacles to their well-being became almost insurmountable. Again, the unusual composition and behaviour of the group lodged at the villa shocked the local inhabitants. Neither George Sand nor Chopin condescended to mix with the Mallorcans and their stay became an unhappy one. He, more than she, felt himself dangerously cut off from civilization and friends. His cough worsened, and suspicions over its exact nature increased. Mallorcan society, justifiably in mortal fear of tuberculosis, treated him as a pariah.

The journey home was frightful. Chopin was spitting blood copiously by the time they reached Barcelona. They took the remainder of the journey in stages designed to alleviate his symptoms and allow him rest. George Sand was a devoted nurse and much of her own time was spent in sparing him the endless visits of well-wishers and the curious. Individually, each was a celebrity enough to raise excitement in any town or city in Europe; together they were an irresistible attraction and they were besieged.

On their eventual return, money matters began to press heavily once again. Buloz began to try to blackmail Sand intellectually into changing her style, with intimations of superior serial contributions to his journal that would undermine her position. One major advantage was gained from this unpleasant brush, however. As a result of Buloz' persuasions, and encouraged by the latter's own new post as Royal Commissioner of the Comédie Française, George Sand was alerted to her own potential as a dramatist and began to write for the theatre.

Chopin, on the other hand, she feared was beginning to show signs of loneliness and restlessness despite her best efforts. The education of her children was occupying a large part of her time and energy, and intuitively she wrote to Chopin's friend Grzymala suggesting that Chopin might be suffering from boredom. Their physical relationship had been already much limited by her knowledge and fear of the results of exertion upon him and her main concern was to establish a routine which taxed him physically as little as possible. In Paris this involved two small households, with George Sand, Maurice and Solange in one, Chopin in the other, and daily meetings between the two.

Her first theatrical efforts were unsuccessful. *Cosima* opened to a barrage of critical abuse and she returned to the novel for security of income. Her subject this time, in *Spiridion*, was inspired by Pierre Leroux, an artisan philosopher whose paper, *Le Globe*, had become the most effective organ of Saint-Simonism. Here again was a man who, like Lammenais and Michel de Bourges, professed to believe more in the perfectibility of human understanding than in the pursuit of excellence. His *De l'humanité*, published in the autumn of 1840 and advocating the replacement of property rights by a new system in which land was both communally owned and managed, appealed greatly to Sand, though her position as a landowner was difficult to sustain in an ideological battle over the role of property. Her writing, entering a new phase, began to reflect a growing faith in the proletariat, and rows with Buloz increased. He accused her of using her talents to propagate 'communistic' ideas. Her espousal of those ideals led to a permanent rift both with Buloz and with Lammenais, who in the same year had published a pamphlet asserting the intellectual superiority of men over women.

Open antagonism was now also being shown to her by Marie d'Agoult, who believed Sand to be pushing Chopin into prominence at Liszt's expense. Chopin did indeed have a brilliant season in 1841 and Sand notes ruefully that he earned more in two hours than she in two months. As a result, Chopin was less dependent on the piano lessons which were his usual source of income. He could now devote more time to composition. During his frequent visits to Nohant, one pupil, to whom he gave daily two-hour lessons, was Solange, of whom he was to grow extremely fond and who was to be one of the main causes of the final rift between himself and her mother. Meanwhile Sand writes to the principal of Solange's school, in a manner which reveals both her ambivalent attitude to Solange and her necessary pre-occupation with the minutiae of day-to-day mothering:

To Sophie Bascans

[Paris, 17? May 1841]

Madame,
This time, Solange has behaved very well with me and since I have to leave around the beginning of next month, I would ask your permission to take her out every Sunday till then, provided she has been good. If not, perhaps you would tell me what she may have done wrong, since I can never get anything out of her.

I have told her off about not taking care of her things. The pretty new hat that she has only put on once before today is already battered. Yet she has a box to put it in at the pension. In her defence, she tells me the woman in charge of clothes will not let her put it in a box and puts it *in a pile* with other things. She would like to have a cupboard for herself and promises to take great care of it. If there is one free, would you be kind enough, Madame, to let her use it? Then we shall see whether she makes proper use of it and if it makes her a little more orderly in her ways.

Mademoiselle de Rosières tells me you think you have overcharged Solange's account by a few centimes. On the contrary, you have undercharged, since I see the bill is for 341fr. 15c.

Some time during this week, if I am feeling better, I shall come and bid you good-day. All last week, I was very ill. I hope Monsieur Bascans and Mademoiselle Zizi give you no such cause for concern.

Very cordially yours,
G.S.

She spent as much time as possible at Nohant where there was a constant stream of visitors. One, the young and brilliant opera singer, Pauline Garcia, much admired by Chopin, was being assiduously courted by none other than Alfred de Musset. Sand took it upon herself to further the suit of his rival, Viardot, with whom she had newly founded *La Revue Indépendante*. This journal was founded to promote the philosophy of the penniless Leroux and included regular contributions from a group of artisan writers and poets from all over France. Its main tenet was its belief in the infinite perfectibility of humankind and the gradual 'passing away' of property in a future where 'laws will regulate inheritance and restrain the right of individuality.' The intrigues leading up to Pauline Garcia's marriage to Viardot formed the basis of Sand's most successful and popular novel, *Consuelo*, published in 1842. Set in eighteenth-century Venice, it tells the story of a young opera singer, Consuelo, of Spanish gipsy extraction, and the trials and tribulations of her career amid the jealousy of her various rivals and the faithlessness of her lover. Its underlying theme is the importance of simplicity and purity in the arts and the uselessness of ostentation and virtuosity. In her own life, this theme echoed the significance to George Sand of the intense feeling behind Chopin's compositions and performances in contrast to the pyrotechnical expertise of Liszt. It was a relatively happy time in Sand's creative life and she urges another old friend to join the 'family' at Nohant:

To Eugene Delacroix

[Nohant, 7 July 1841]

I found the lighter in a big shop selling fancy goods almost in the middle of the gallery on the Théâtre Français, Théâtre Palais-Royal side. The shop has two glass doors and a big selection of boxes, wallets, travel goods and all kinds of rubbish. It's the only one of the kind that has two doors. I can't give you any more details except that it's a name with *on* in it, Garnesson or Cabasson, or Paillason or Pantalon – or something. I don't know if you'll find another lighter like it. The lighter was the only one in the shop, and in the whole of the Palais Royal.

Now you mustn't be too happy with your brother, my dear old pal, or you'll not need any friendship from us. I want you to know that Pauline is coming to Nohant in August. I've just had a letter from her, promising faithfully. Imagine being in the country with both Pauline and Chip Chip, that will really be something. Plus of course myself, who loves you dearly, and it's always very nice to be loved. Maurice who still adores you, swears by you in fact, is daubing all day long. All the same he does seem to be making some fitful progress, I think. As for me, I've been tempted to take up an old passion of mine, almost as silly as fishing, and that's watercolours of flowers. However I am forced to abstain from such degeneracy for I have to finish *my poor little novel** which is only limping along and much disturbed by horses and dogs.

Monsieur Pistolet is a great favourite – I must say he's

*Horace.

the most extraordinary creature, as wonderfully
Napoleonic as *L'Amour*. He'll spring from a peak
hundreds of feet high, speed like an arrow over stones,
thorns, lakes, everything, to plunge into the river after
stones as big as himself. He brings them out, carries them
back so boldly and with such enthusiasm, that all the
men and dogs around are lost in admiration. He swims
like a fish, and drags out whole saplings from the river. It
has to be seen to be believed. Please respond to this
biographical extract with a bulletin on the deeds and
derring-do of L'Amour and Jenny.

One other little domestic detail. We have had an
earthquake here, the second in thirty years. So I shall
have been through two without stirring from my own
very flat, very unvolcanic village. You'll have to go much
further if you want to find real wonders of the world.
Ours, it must be admitted, was not as violent as the one
in Martinique. Not so much as a tile broken. But I can
tell you, it's quite a surprise when you're stretched out
comfortably on your sofa, on a beautifully calm moonlit
night, to feel yourself suddenly lifted up and shaken a
few times as if somebody were playing jokes on you from
under the bed. And at the same time the walls shook and
the paintings thudded against them. There was a sinister
rumbling sound and then suddenly the moon darkened.
All at once there seemed to be a great veil covering the
sky and it was so hot you could hardly breathe. The
whole of nature seemed horribly desolate, silent and *dead*.
Pistolet was barking, my brother's horned friends were
lowing and Chopin's poor nerves, as the old Rancogne
song goes, were shattered and in tatters. The peasants
round here thought the devil had a hand in it. It was
midnight, the moon was full and at that precise moment I
turned thirty-seven years old – which proves I'm not a
lunatic for nothing. At 2 o'clock in the morning there was
a dreadful storm, and some renewed shuddering, wind

and lightning and a deluge of water from a cloudless sky. For three days now the weather has been appalling, but it's because of the earthquake. When you come, it will all be over, I promise you. If, however, you would like to see an earthquake, since it's fairly unusual, we shall do our best to put one on for you. Just give us time and we shall have it all arranged.

So do come, dear and good friend. We are counting so much on having you here it would be a real disappointment if you did not. Everyone here adores you and they ask me to embrace you for them. Many many hugs therefore.

George*

Maurice's interest in painting was developing and Sand was able eventually to send him off for training in Delacroix' *atelier* in Paris. Solange's education proved to be a more difficult problem and her concerns over it are interesting, amongst other things, for the light they shed on Sand's views on work:

To Fernand Bascans

[Nohant, 29 Sept 1841]

I am very late in replying to your kind letter. This is because I wished before doing so to assess Solange's intellectual progress and her moral development so as to be able to discuss both with you. This was initially impossible in the fever of excitement which possesses her here at the moment and which must be allowed to run its necessary course. However, I have managed to do a little, albeit in fits and starts (and, *vis à vis* her studies, through surprise tactics). Though no more even-tempered, I have

---

*Pauline: Pauline Garcia. Chip-Chip: Chopin. Monsieur Pistolet: George Sand's dog. *L'Amour*: Delacroix's cat. Jenny: a servant in Delacroix's *atelier*.

found her capable of greater restraint and self-discipline than before. And though there is still a long way to go on that score, I can see that your labours have not been in vain and I am full of hope.

As far as her studies are concerned I shall tell you exactly what my impressions are. Everything which she has learned from you in private lessons has been perfectly understood and retained with miraculously detailed accuracy! Her great strength is in the memorizing of facts. She can express them, I believe she understands them properly, she can analyse them logically and write with some talent; in other words she could do well in history. Beyond that, I see nothing artistic in her nature; this is unimportant. She must be developed according to her aptitude. I must thank you for already having gone far in this direction, for she has learnt a great deal in the short time you have had her under your wing. Despite loud protestation that she does not care or cannot be bothered, I can see she has developed a taste for and a pride in the work you have given her to do. I am therefore extremely desirous that she continue her private lessons with you, and that you give her a good deal to read and to write with you: the cornerstone of her education consists in this. Outside this domain, I know there is little to be done for Solange; I know that in the general classes, of four or five students, in which no girl is separately and thoroughly tested, she will learn nothing. These general classes are good if one has the desire to listen; the majority of children, and Solange is no exception, do not have this desire. Thus English lessons are a waste of time for her (I shall return to this subject later on) and are positively harmful to her mind. But *as a whole*, general classes have a value different from real and rapid intellectual progress. They teach personal discipline over the mind and body. For this reason, general classes do seem necessary for my daughter who could otherwise be led astray by her proud and wilful temperament and into some very eccentric ways of behaving. So although these lessons are good for her in moral terms, in intellectual terms they produce practically nothing. Since it is important that both these faculties be developed simultaneously, Solange cannot do without good and forceful private tuition given as often and for as long as possible. So I have the following plan to put forward to you. Instead of attending those classes in which she does nothing, she should come to you, to read, and do tracts and resumés of texts. If that cannot be arranged, then at least let her have a little spot where she can work away on her history, so that she can give you an exact account of what she has been doing.

These times would seem to be the hours of English classes, the pitiful results of which will not do. This is not the consequence of a *complaint* of Solange's; I have delved very carefully into the recesses of her mind, and have taken into account her own laziness. Using the wiles of a seasoned lawyer I have examined the method used in this kind of teaching and I am certain that the means of surveillance is what is at fault here. The students may choose not only not to *hear* (and a teacher can do nothing about that) but also not to *listen*. I do not believe Solange feels any hostility towards the English mistress. In fact she says that during break this teacher can get her to make some progress but that after it, there is no way Solange can catch up with what she has not learned, or upon knowledge of which she has not been tested and with which she has been given no help whatsoever. She has, without question, forgotten every single word of the little she ever knew in this subject. This gives me no cause for regret, I am not over-anxious that she learn English; if she comes to find it useful one day, she can take it up then. What I *am* anxious for her to do is to *learn how to work*. For although a good, satisfying lesson cannot always produce an appetite for work and the means of completing it, a slightly sloppy or unenthusiastically given lesson is sure to remove both the desire for and the intention to accomplish work. Solange will always try and shake off the shackles if they are loosely bound and if a teacher is the slightest bit absent-minded or not feeling very well or easy-going, her contempt for study reaches even further depths. Other general lessons, French in particular, seem to me to be very good, she has certainly benefited from them and made great progress in this field. So, in conclusion, if it were possible for you to substitute for English, lessons in French *of a literary kind*, or in history *of a philosophical kind*, as has already been very successfully done, there would be great improvement. I am sure that you have more than enough to do as it is and I should not dare to ask you to increase your heavy load. But if there were, in your circle, someone who could hear her go over the history lessons you give her, I should be happy to reimburse those labours with whatever you judged appropriate: they would be under your general direction and follow your method exactly so that your private lessons, the educational good seed upon which I set so much store, should fall on soil laboured well enough to receive it.

I am asking a great deal, I'm sure, but I know you will help me in the difficult work of cultivating this hard terrain. She told me about the life of Francis I, having remembered every detail of it; including places, dates and even strategy. A memory like hers is capable of carrying a great store of knowledge and it would be a pity not to feed it with one of the most importantly maturing of educational factors, the study of *history*.

A thousand pardons for all these lengthy and detailed remarks. I hope that the English mistress will not be reprimanded on our account, nor even learn how ungrateful Solange is to her for her great sweetness. Her lessons are no doubt well adapted to gentler and calmer natures than my *prima donna*. So this letter should not be construed as telling tales or complaining; I have given enough lessons in my time to know that teaching is the most demanding and the most difficult of jobs. I have lived long enough to know that one cannot ask for the impossible, or go beyond a certain limit of excellence in all things. I very much appreciate the exemplary organization of your establishment and I am both pleased with and grateful for the results it produces. Solange seems to me to be full of respect for you and affection towards Madame Bascans, and this is a great thing. She has a jealous nature and seemed very anxious to monopolize the affections of Madame Bascans. In her relation with me she is quick to take offence; this is one of her weaknesses (indeed, this tendency would become monstrous if I were to allow it). I can see it could develop into a passionate attachment to your wife, and Madame Bascans, were she to show preference elsewhere, should guard against a violent reaction on Solange's part.

I shall send her back to you as soon as possible, around the time of the proper beginning of term, in eight to ten days or so, I believe. I may have to keep her here a few days longer should the business affairs of my brother, who is to bring her back, detain him. We are somewhat remote here, and very busy; we cannot always fit in what we should like. Since you ask for news of my own work, I can tell you that I have recently completed a large, heavy novel, which began as full of good intentions as ever.* Would that the results were so fine. But I am not discouraged by such a little thing as this. My works provide merely temporary amusement and will die with me. All they can do and all I wish them to do during

*Horace.

these times of struggle and uncertainty, which will pass also, is sustain the dream of finer feelings in stronger, more effective people than myself.

Do believe that your good opinion and your concern are very sweetly encouraging to me. Remember me very kindly to you all; with affectionate best wishes.

Yours,

George Sand

For the past week or so Solange has been writing a letter for Madame Bascans, and another two for friends who have written to her. But so many excitements, butterflies, puppies and the rest, occupy her little mind these days that I dare not wait to include hers with this letter.

George Sand was no less concerned for the health of her relationship with Chopin who was growing sadder as news of losses in his native Poland reached his ears. It was six years since he and George Sand had begun to see each other every day and she had become increasingly worried that the strain of their physical relationship would be detrimental to his delicate constitution. She was able to share her anxieties over his health with his sister, when she visited Nohant for the first time soon after the death of Chopin's father. Coming, as it did, only two years after the death from pulmonary tuberculosis of his closest friend, the loss affected him deeply.

In November 1845, Chopin returned from Nohant to Paris alone for the first time. Sand, whose maternal instinct was strongly developed, was preoccupied with a new recruit to the Nohant family household – Augustine Brault, the daughter of a third cousin on her mother's side, whom George Sand had helped financially over the years. Well-meaning though this act of generosity was, and badly needed, since the girl was subject to physical violence in her own home, it aroused the profound jealousy of Solange and set in motion a sequence of events that ended in great bitterness.

As was natural, once the novelty of having a new sister wore off, Solange began to feel dispossessed. Both girls were reaching marriageable age and there was rivalry between them, not so much over one particular suitor as over their general desirability. Chopin disapproved very strongly of Solange's eventual choice of husband, the sculptor Auguste Clésinger. George Sand however, gave her approval, refusing to heed the warnings of either Chopin or those other artists who knew his reputation as a brute. The fastidious Chopin in the meantime had been alienated by the influence over George Sand of her 'radical' friends, whom he considered uncouth. Many of George Sand's circle believed that she was pushing a difficult daughter into a marriage that would tame her.

Clésinger turned out to be a ruthless opportunist. Already heavily in debt, he imagined that marriage to the famous author's daughter would be the end of his financial troubles. Solange, once married, began to put on airs at the expense both of her cousin Augustine and of her mother, harrassing both at Nohant with her husband in tow. Disappointed in his expectation, Clésinger turned at first surly then violent. During one of their confrontations there, the new son-in-law came to blows not only with the male members of the household, but with George Sand herself. Claiming illness, and writing urgently to Chopin for the loan refused by Sand of his *calèche*, Solange received a letter by return, authorizing her to use it. This was the last straw for Sand. A strong bond was established between Chopin and 'Sol', as relations between mother and daughter soured. Effectively this was the end of relations between Chopin and Sand. A very large part of their correspondence was destroyed but, after his death, pressed amongst his most precious possessions was found George Sand's first note to him after hearing him play. It read *'On vous adore'* ('We adore you').

The loss of Chopin was a kind of breaking point in Sand's life. She wrote less enthusiastically now and felt herself aged beyond her years. In a mood of nostalgia, she began *L'Histoire de ma vie*, recounting in vivid detail the family stories told to her by her grandmother. These stories linked the latter's pre-Revolutionary youth with George Sand's middle years for suddenly, on the political front, there was a violent eruption which put her more personal matters in a slightly different perspective.

For some time, in *La Revue Indépendante*, Sand had been promoting the literary work of a relatively uneducated group of proletarian writers and poets; Magu a weaver, Reboul a baker, Jasmin a barber and Charles Poncy the Toulon mason to whom *Marianne* is dedicated, were all represented in its pages. Her socialism had expressed itself in her own novels also: *Horace, Le Meunier d'Angibault, Jeanne* and *Le Compagnon du tour de France* had taken as their subjects the proletariat of the cities and the countryside. It was these novels to which Dostoevsky was referring when he named George Sand as one of the greatest champions of 'the cause'.

Deep-rooted as her hostility to the Louis-Philippe monarchy had been, Sand, like others in February 1848, was surprised by the suddenness of the events which were soon to shake and topple it. The Republic of which she and her associates had been dreaming seemed much closer at hand than had at first seemed possible. After eight years of dull and uninspired government based on the principle of private enrichment, France was in a mood for change. The economic gap between the pay of the average worker and the huge incomes to be derived from speculative investment in new industrial development, like the railway, was vast and obvious. Successive poor harvests in the preceding two years had raised the price of food to intolerable levels. In February, relatively peaceful opposition to the government soon gave way to rioting and the erection of barricades in Paris.

Overjoyed, Sand threw herself into the fray, as Louis-Philippe abdicated and fled to England, and Lamartine the poet-diplomat formed a government in his place. Louis Blanc, an old friend of Sand's, whipped up a mob demanding the proclamation of a new republic. From Nohant, Sand travelled as the head of a delegation of local republicans to express their support in whatever way they could. Signing herself with her old name, as she always did in correspondence with him, Sand wrote to her cousin at Chenonceaux:

To René Vallet de Villeneuve

[Paris, Saturday night 4 March 1848]

I hope you are neither sad nor worried. We should have no regrets for what we have swept away. We shall plunge into the unknown with hope and faith. I say the unknown for neither party in the present republic is likely to be so wrong-minded and misled as others you have lived through. The gentle courage of the people was wonderful to behold and, *generally speaking*, power is in the hands of good and honest men. I have come to discover this for myself, since I am closely connected with several of them; I shall return to Nohant tomorrow with the certain knowledge that they have the best intentions in the world and will do the best they can. We should be grateful to them for not having allowed these bloody struggles to become protracted; the rich should be grateful to them for having inspired a sense of calm and confidence in the poorer classes. I am writing to you in some haste in order to reassure you in case you should be entertaining fears during these times. I know *better than anyone* what is happening both at government and at street level. Everything is safe and sure, apart from a few exceptions; these exceptions are effectively restrained by a vast majority. I hope my cousin does not curse us. The sanctity of the church was respected and the cross was carried in the middle of the triumphant crowd. This morning the archbishop of Paris blessed the tomb of our unknown soldier. We were merciful to our true enemies, when captive, and gave them safe conduct to escape. Burn this letter; this last information could have very serious implications if known.

Love me as before, despite my being a *republican*. And I, in turn, hold you dearer than ever.

Aurore

It was during the hectic days which followed that, bumping into Chopin by chance, she learned that Solange had just given birth to a baby girl. On the political front, she wrote an impassioned congratulatory *Lettre au Peuple* (*Letter to the People*), published privately, and, in the provincial elections following the abdication, proposed 'affirmative action' in favour of one worker and one peasant per department, to offset the otherwise inevitable ascendancy, once again, of the literate bourgeoisie.

By this time, George Sand was one of the most well-known, influential and articulate women in France. She was seen as a natural choice to play a leading role in the development of the Republic. It was at this time that she effectively refused the symbolic title of 'Muse of the Republic', which later became known popularly as 'the Marianne'. The name was the password of a secret society formed after 1851 whose aim was the toppling of the government; its origin may go even further back, to the days of the Terror, when it had represented a prostitute impersonating the Goddess of Reason. In refusing this leading role and association with the object of men's ambitions, she paved the way for a radically different definition of a feminine ideal. Unbeknown to her, her name had been included on a list of forty candidates for election to the National Assembly. In a passionate declaration, she rejected this. For women to enter official and bureaucratic politics before they had shaken off the causes of their own real oppression, she saw as either a blind or a trap:

To Members of the Central Committee

[Paris, mid-April 1848]

I do not thank you for having included my name on some forty or so Central Committee lists. I cannot believe you would wish me to do something I should never dream of and sail under impossibly false colours. You wish to see established a principle adopted by yourselves, apparently, and I feel the time has come for me to present certain considerations to you concerning this same principle which needs now to be carefully discussed and evaluated.

Should women one day participate in political life? Yes; like you, I believe so, but is that day close at hand? No, I think not. In order for the condition of women to be so transformed, society must be transformed radically.

On these two points, we are perhaps already agreed. But there is a third to consider. Some women have put the following question: In order for society to be transformed, should not women take part immediately in public affairs? – I dare reply that they ought not, since social conditions are such that women can not in all honesty and in all loyalty to each other fulfil a political mandate yet.

Since marriage implies her tutelage to and dependence upon a man, it is impossible for any woman to possess political independence until, as an individual, she breaks the laws of custom and habit which keep that tutelage sacrosanct.

I apologize to those of my own sex who think differently about this issue but I believe it is senseless to put the cart before the horse and finish at the beginning of what there is to be done. And let us understand perfectly how much time, how much thought and how much new enlightenment concerning present morality is necessary before such a beginning can take place.

Should I even agree on a point of departure with those who call for women's suffrage? I think not, and I think we should understand each other very clearly on this essential point.

What do these ladies mean by women's suffrage? Do they mean what Saint-Simon, Enfantin and Fourier mean? Do they wish to destroy the institution of marriage and advocate promiscuity? If so (and all power to them), I shall find their claims to political life very logical. I should, however, dissociate myself personally from them and from their cause which becomes in this respect alien to me. So, I have nothing more to say. I make no response. I have no argument to make. I distance myself and I leave it to public morality to deal with this regrettable fantasy. You must understand, citizens, that I cannot feel the slightest solidarity with you on an issue upon which I have not been consulted. Your votes are an insult and I appeal to your consciences for having cast them for me without my knowledge.

But I cannot believe this is what they are claiming. It would give too much credence to those who castigate socialists for wanting to destroy the family. No, no, those women who have unwisely brought up the question of their political rights are not, when they come to you for your votes, hiding in the folds of their shawls some filthy Fourierist doctrine, some esoteric, promiscuous nonsense of that kind. If, as I believe, they do not wish to destroy the sanctity of earthly love, they want to prove they possess the same logic and judgement as men through a somewhat risky *electoral campaign.*

So that there should be no ambiguity on these points, I should like to speak my mind freely on the popular theme of the emancipation of women, which is so much discussed these days.

I believe this emancipation could be easily and immediately brought about to the extent that our present state of morals allows. It would consist simply in giving back to the woman all the civil rights which marriage alone takes from her, and which she may preserve only by remaining unmarried. This is a loathsome deficiency in our legislation. It places the woman entirely under the grasping domination of the man and makes marriage for her a condition of everlasting minority. Most young girls would decide never to marry if they had the slightest knowledge of civil law at the age when they give up their rights. It is curious that the advocates of the old order of things are at pains to make the words *family* and *property* figure in their mendacious propaganda; the admirable pact of marriage as they understand it destroys forever all the property rights of an entire sex. Either property is not the sacred thing they proclaim or marriage is not the equally sacred thing. Two sacred things can only destroy each other.

I am certain that this reform is quite possible in the near future. It is one of the first questions with which a socialist republic should be concerned. I do not think it would be in the least bit harmful to conjugal faithfulness or to good, harmonious domestic relations, unless one regards equality as a condition of disorder and discord.

We believe the opposite and humanity has always believed likewise.

But it is asked where will the principal authority necessary to the existence of the family reside if it is shared equally by father and by mother. We say that authority should not be immobilized in the person of someone who could without impunity act wrongly always, but that it should pass freely from one to the other according to the dictates of feeling and reason. When the interests of children were in question I do not see why confidence should not be placed in the care of the mother, who is recognized to have the stronger and more constant love of her progeniture. As for the rest, when it is asked how a conjugal association could subsist where the husband is not the head, the absolute and final arbiter, it is a little like asking how the free man could get along without a master, or a republic without a king. The principle of individual and unlimited authority is disappearing like the principle of divine law and men are not generally so wicked towards their wives as some of them so often tell us. This may be true once or twice in a lifetime but they would be closer to what is fair and true if they recognized that the majority of men are in fact, these days, anxious to make conjugal equality the basis of their happiness. Not all of them are logical enough to recognize in theory an equality which, in practice, in their homes, they would be loath to destroy, but it has passed into our customs and the man who mistreats and humiliates his partner is not honoured among other men. Until the law sanctions this civil equality it is certain that intolerable abuses of marital authority will continue to subsist. It is also certain that the mother, still a minor at the age of eighty, is in a ridiculous and humiliating situation. It is only a despotic law which now gives to the husband the right to withhold the material conditions necessary for the welfare of his wife and children, gives him the right to commit adulterous affairs outside the conjugal home, the right to murder his wife if she is unfaithful, the right to exclude his wife from the education of their children, to corrupt them through bad example and erroneous principles, by appointing his mistresses their governesses, as we see happen in some illustrious families; it gives him the right of command over the entire household, to instruct domestic staff, including maids, to insult the mother; to throw out the wife's parents and install his own for her to look after; the right to reduce her to poverty while he spends the capital that belongs to her on other women; the right to beat her and to have her complaints rejected by a court of law if she cannot produce witnesses or if she is afraid of scandal; and finally the right to dishonour her name with groundless insinuations and to have her punished for the mistakes she makes. These savage, atrocious, anti-human laws are the sole causes, I venture, of all the infidelities, the quarrels, the scandals and the crimes which so often sully the sanctuary of the family, and which will continue to sully it, poor human beings that we are, until you destroy at one and the same time, the scaffold and the ball and chain for the criminal, and insult and domestic slavery, prison and public shame for the unfaithful woman. Until such a time comes, women will be prey to the vices of all oppressed people, and be reduced to using the wiles of the slave. Those of you who do not become tyrants will remain what so many of you are today, the ridiculous slaves of other slaves bent on revenge.

Yes, woman is a slave in principle and this is because she is beginning to emerge from slavery in fact. For her, now, there is hardly any point between exasperating servitude or a tyranny which belittles her husband. The time has come to recognize in principle her rights to civil equality and to have this principle enshrined in the constitutional and social developments which are soon, let us hope, to take place. In this respect the law will only be keeping abreast of custom; in the vast majority of homes, it is the woman who rules, and it is wrong for this authority to be seen as having been gained by a determined use of wiliness and cunning. The law is behind the times. Wives have been corrupted by usurpation of an authority wrongly denied to them and which they can never legally recover. The man who is a slave may openly and honestly revolt against his master in an attempt to regain his freedom and his dignity. The woman who is a slave may only deceive her master and gain a hollow victory through slyness and deceit.

What, in fact, is that liberty she may gain, albeit fraudulently? It is adultery. And what kind of dignity may she pride herself on possessing without her husband's knowledge? A gain in ascendancy that makes both her and him ridiculous. These abuses must stop and the good husband no longer be seen as a foolish dupe laughed at by his wife and friends. Equally, a woman who is gentle, loyal and dutiful ought not to be viewed as the victim of her own devotion, to be tyrannized and exploited at will. Lastly, a woman who one day does get carried away should not be branded and publicly punished, dishonoured in the eyes of her children, placed outside the pale and forced to hate him who chastises and shames her foreever.

The punishment of adultery, one of the most serious and least seriously considered questions whose importance cannot be too greatly stressed, the punishment of adultery is a brutal law designed to perpetuate and increase adultery itself. Adultery is its own punishment, it carries its own remorse and its own unutterable regret. It should be sufficient cause for divorce or separation if it causes unbearable offence. But this law, which allows a man to take back the dishonoured wife he himself has put in prison, this law which forces the woman to return and

suffer the slow torture of her own degradation and to
suffer this at all times, and in the presence of her
children, this is an infamous and odious law which does
far greater dishonour to the man who uses it than to the
woman it seeks to break.

It is the law of personal hatred and vengeance. The
results of its application are scandal, family shame and an
ineradicable smear on the name of the children. It is no
less inhuman than the law which allows a husband to kill
a wife caught in *flagrante delicto* or the law which permits
men in the East to tie their women into sacks and throw
them down a well or into the sea. Death would be
nothing compared to a life of slavery, in which a woman
is condemned to suffer the embraces of a master who has
trodden her underfoot.

So, civil equality, equality in marriage, equality in the
family, this is what you can and what you must seek and
demand . . .

George Sand's foremost hope from a socialist republic was
the abolition of male dominance in the private as well as the
public sphere. It is clear from this letter that she believed
true reform in the personal domain to be a prerequisite rather
than a consequence of genuine political reform and that the
most effective means of achieving both was through
education.

Her involvement in the 1848 Revolution ended abruptly
when, after months of ceaseless activity, she witnessed the
temporary victory of the moderates. She was revolted by the
renewed violence and bloodshed, similar to her early days in
Paris when she had been sickened by the stench of corpses
from the morgue opposite her apartments, and the sight of
blood running into the Seine. As the insurrection was put
down eventually by the National Guard, she came to the
conclusion that people are never changed by violence. She

placed higher hopes from then on in the value of words and peaceful action.

Her sadness was further increased the following year by the death of Marie Dorval, for whose family she also took considerable financial responsibility; and, five months later, by that of her beloved Chopin. These losses moved her to write in a different genre and a calmer style. Her stage adaptation of her novel, *François le Champi*, was highly successful and her preference, as she grew older, was to reach a vaster public through the theatre than that privileged through literacy.

In 1851 Louis Napoléon staged a *coup d'état* and a number of prominent republicans were arrested. As rumours of her own imminent arrest reached her, George Sand decided that attack was the best means of defence. Taking the initiative, she sought an interview with the Prince himself. Like so many others, he was already a great admirer of her work, having read *Mauprat* and *Consuelo* in particular with much enthusiasm. She pleaded eloquently for an amnesty and a cessation of the arrests taking place. From then until December of 1852 she worked ceaselessly to have sentences commuted, deportation orders lifted, and by direct appeal and intercession managed to achieve a degree of leniency or clemency for most of those who asked for her help.

[Paris, 12 Feb 1852]

Prince,

Allow me to place before your eyes a sad letter of supplication from 4 soldiers condemned to death who, in their deep ignorance of political matters, chose a blacklisted person as their intermediary. The wife of this man, who neither asks nor hopes for any alleviation of her own suffering and does not know the four signatories any better than I do, has sent me their letter together with some beautiful lines of her own; her words will touch you more deeply, I am sure, than any pleading on my part. This poor unfortunate worker who with her three children is reduced to penury, sick herself, but uncomplaining and resigned, would never believe I might dare to ask you yourself to read her misspelt efforts. Nor would I have dreamed of importuning you until I saw that it was a question of life or death and not simply another of my party's problems. I know that a moment's hesitation would rid me of the little sleep which is given me.

Nor could I refuse to represent the plea of the unfortunate Emile Roget . . .

Sand's political disenchantment coincided with a renewed interest in the Berry, and more time spent with her family. A temporary truce had been called with Solange, whose five-year-old daughter, Nini, became the apple of Sand's eye. Solange and Clésinger were on the point of separation; until legal custody was granted to one or other parent, the child was obliged to remain at her school. Here, in 1855, she contracted scarlet fever; after nearly a week, while the headmistress decided whether or not to entrust her to Solange's care, Nini was sent home to Nohant, where she died. George Sand's grief knew no bounds. She found herself incapable of working and, when she did resume, it was to write the vengeful *Elle et Lui*, based on her affair in Venice with Musset,* twenty years earlier.

Meanwhile, English xenophobia expressed itself eloquently as Sand's novels grew more popular:

We are told there is a steady demand amongst 'our upper classes' for what is especially understood by French novels – particularly those of George Sand – and one that

---

*In his introduction to George Sand's *Correspondance* (Editions Garnier-Frères, 1964–85), Georges Lubin comments that he had presumed hostilities between the Musset and Sand factions must have died down by now and was surprised to find them continuing vigorously to this day.

keeps its ground, though time has worn out their authors' power for new mischief. Where people live for excitement, we can scarcely hope to dissuade them from seeking it wherever it is to be found; but warning and remonstrance may be of service where the old defences have not yet given way, as we believe they have not, in the heart of quiet English society . . . Words expressive of admiration, love, reverence, in a Christian tongue, are all connected with ideas of faith and purity. If George Sand wants to excite our sympathy, and inspire our admiration for persons and things of a wholly opposite character, she has only the old words to express them in, and hence an inevitable confusion. If she had a choice, we believe that she would have kept clear of what we must call a profanation; but she could not coin words, and all those *we* should call appropriate would simply defeat her end. Taking such words, then as *religion, nature, Dieu, Ciel, Providence, conscience, vertu, austerité, pudeur, chastité* (sic), *pur, maternel,* &cetera, do we not feel that 'Some rude hand has smutched them'?

Does she not degrade our vocabulary?

Dumas *père* and *fils* joined her circle at this time, as did the brothers Jules and Edmond de Goncourt and Maxime du Camp, but their company was nowhere near as lively as the earlier group of 'Fellows'. Her son Maurice married and produced a little son Marc-Antoine, but he too died in infancy.

The sadness which threatened to permeate the last ten years of George Sand's life was lifted to a large extent by the friendships she continued to make, not least with Gustave Flaubert. Before the publication of his Carthaginian novel *Salammbô*, they had never met and Flaubert had been antipathetic to what he termed her 'inadmissible doctrines'.

Their attitude towards literature could not have been more fundamentally opposed; he a firm believer in art for art's sake, and she equally convinced of its functionalist role in the forming of social values. Agreeably surprised by the generous review she wrote of his novel, he had written to thank her and by 1866 their friendship was sufficiently well established for each to visit the other's home. Flaubert wrote asking for a picture of her, which she duly dispatched:

Flaubert to George Sand

[Croisset, Saturday night . . . 1866]

So I've got it at last, a portrait of that dear, lovely and illustrious face of yours! I shall have a large frame made for it and hang it on the wall of my room. I shall then be able to say, as Talleyrand did to Louis-Philippe: 'This is the greatest honour ever bestowed on my house'. Not such an apt quotation, come to think of it; we're better than either of those two fellows any day.

Of the two, the one I prefer is the drawing by Couture. Marchal has seen only 'the good woman' in you. Old romantic as I am, what I see in the other is the 'portrait of the author' who wove such dreams for me in my youth . . .

As the friendship developed, she became his grammatically ambivalent *chère maître*, and they became to each other 'old troubadour'. Their letters became a source of great comfort to each other:

Flaubert to George Sand

[Croisset, Tuesday . . . 1866]

There you are feeling sad and lonely, you say, and here am I feeling the same way. Where do they come from, do you think, these black moods that engulf us like this? They rise like a tide, you feel as if you are drowning and you have to escape somehow. What I do is lie, floating, letting it all wash over me.

My novel* has been going very badly this last little while. On top of that, news of several deaths. Cormentin (a friend for over twenty-five years), Gavarni, and others besides but things will get better. You, of course, have no idea what it's like to spend the whole day with your head in your hands, trying to squeeze the right word out of your miserable brain. Ideas flow in you constantly, bountifully, like a river. All I have is a thin little trickle and I have to work mightily at my art to get any sparkle at all out of it. I know all about the *anguish* of style I can tell you! My whole time is spent worrying something out of my head or my heart and that, in a nutshell, is the life-story of your friend here. You ask if he sometimes spares a thought for his old troubadour. I should think so indeed! And he misses her. Those midnight talks of ours were so lovely. There were times when I could hardly stop myself from coming over and kissing you (big baby that I am).

Your ears must have been burning last night. I was with all the family having dinner at my brother's. We talked about hardly anything else except you of course, I tore you to shreds, my beloved *maître*. By the way (same train of thought), about your last letter; I've just been reading old Montaigne's 'On some lines of Virgil'. What he has to say about chastity are my own thoughts entirely. It is the effort behind it which is good, not the abstinence itself. Otherwise you might just as well do as the Catholics and condemn the flesh outright and God knows what that leads to! So at the risk of repeating

*L'Éducation sentimale.

myself and of being a real Prudhomme I'll say your young man is wrong. If he is chaste at twenty he will be a dirty old roué by the age of fifty.

Spend! Be profligate! All great souls, that's to say all good ones, expend all their energies regardless of the cost. You must suffer and enjoy, laugh, cry, love and work, in other words you must let every fibre of your being thrill with life. That's the meaning of being human, I think . . .

George Sand was moved to reflect on the nature of her friendship for him:

George Sand to Flaubert

[Nohant, 15 January 1867]

. . . I have just received your letter this morning, dear friend of my heart. Why is it, I wonder, that I love you more than all the others, more even than old friends, tried and true? . . . I will tell you what I think it is. When you are old, enjoying the evening of your life, which is the most beautiful and subtly lit of all stages, you see everything, especially affection, in a new light.

When your personality is at the height of its powers, you feel friendship as you feel ground, that's to say for what it can contribute in terms of solidity. As you yourself feel solid, you want to know that what carries you or what leads you is solid also. But when the intensity of the *self* is dissipated, you love people and things for what they are in themselves, for what they represent in the eye of your soul and not what they bring or add to your own self.

Friendship then is like a statue or a painting which you would long to own if only you had a beautiful home in which to place it. You know all the time that, like the proverbial rolling stone, you will have passed through life without gathering any moss, that you will always be a true bohemian, a sentimental troubadour. You know you will always be like that and that you'll die with neither hearth nor home to call your own. So when you think of the statue or the picture that you would not know what to do with, lacking a place of honour in which to put it, you are happy to think of it in some place of worship, far away from the bright glare of cold analysis. You like to think of it a little distant from you yourself and you love it all the more in consequence. You say to yourself you will be able to return to it, see it again and always understand it. It will not have been altered by contact with your personality. It will not be yourself in it that you love.

And that, truly is how the ideal, which you can never hold, is held within you, because it remains *itself*. That is the whole secret of beauty, of truth, of love, friendship, art, faith and inspiration. Think about it and you will see . . .

Though he had lost his first son, Maurice's family was now growing and George Sand was delighted to send Flaubert portraits of her grandchildren. Writing to thank her for them, Flaubert takes issue with her opinion of the events now taking place in the wake of the Franco-Prussian war. The Parisian population had been reduced to starvation by the Prussians and eventually surrendered. In Flaubert's view, this was typically ignoble of its leaders, who afterwards returned a cautious government bent on reconciliation. Sand believed the avoidance of further bloodshed to be the most important objective and had been horrified by rumours of an impending revolution, as a result of mounting public indignation against the government.

Flaubert to George Sand

[Croisset, 8 September 1871]

Oh, aren't they beautiful! What little darlings, what sweet, gentle faces! My mother was very touched and so was I. It was a really kind thought of yours to send them and I thank you very much indeed. I do envy Maurice. His life is nothing like as arid as mine is here. Your letter and mine crossed again. It proves without doubt that we feel the same things at the same time and to the same degree.

What makes you so sad? This is nothing new. Humanity has always been the same and I believe the mass, the herd, will always be despicable. The only thing that matters is having a small group of like-minded spirits to pass on the torch to each other. As long as mandarins command no respect, as long as the Academy of Science does not take the place of the Pope, the whole of politics, the whole of society down to its very roots will remain always and forever a ludicrous and disgusting pile of old rubbish.

We are floundering about in the aftermath of a revolution which was itself a failure, an aborted coup, a mess, whichever way you look at it. And the reason is because it was rooted in Christianity and mediaeval thinking. The idea of equality (which is all modern democracy is) is an essential Christian idea quite contrary to the idea of justice. Just look at how much feeling counts for these days and see how little value is placed on the idea of obligation. Murder is no longer scandalous and those who set fire to Paris get off more lightly than the detractors of Monsieur Favre.* If France is ever to rise again she must abandon inspiration in favour of the sciences and let a critical examination of things take the place of all the metaphysics you like. I am sure we will

*Jules Favre, 1809–80, barrister, deputy and later foreign minister.

seem like idiots to posterity. The words 'republic' and
'monarchy' will be as amusing to them as the words
'realism' and 'nominalism' are to us today. I defy anyone
to show me any difference whatsoever between them. A
modern republic and a constitutional monarchy are
identical. Yet people will argue and yell and fight over
them both . . .

The first step on the road to recovery would be to get
rid of that insult to human intelligence, universal
suffrage. As it is now constituted, one element prevails,
to the detriment of all others; number takes precedence
over mind, education, race and even money, all of which
count for more than sheer numbers. Society, which
always has to have some sort of protective God or
Saviour, is probably not capable of defending itself
against this. The conservative party does not even possess
that brute instinct which will at least put up a fight to
protect hide and home. It will be split up by
internationals, the Jesuits of the future. But as in the
past, with neither homeland nor the thirst for justice,
they will never succeed. The International will founder
because it is wrong. It has no ideals. It has only envy.

Oh, *chère bon maître*, if only you could hate. That is
what has always been missing in you; hatred. Your big
sphinx-like eyes have viewed the world through a golden
haze. It came from the sun in your heart. Now, so many
shadows have risen that you no longer recognize things.
Rise! Cry! Thunder against them! Lift up your great lyre
of bronze and summon us! At the sound of it, the
monsters will flee. Sprinkle on us drops of wounded
Themis' blood, still unavenged.

Why do you feel that 'strong bonds have been broken'?
What could be broken? Your bonds are indestructible and
your love linked to the eternal. It is our ignorance of
history that makes us despair of our own times.
Humanity has always been like this. We were simply

lulled by a few years' peace, that's all. I too once believed in the perfectibility of man but we should be strictly honest and value our own times no more highly than those of Pericles or Shakespeare – appalling periods when beautiful things were accomplished. Tell me you will lift your head again and that you will be thinking of your old troubadour who adores you.

George Sand's reply was a *cri de coeur*:

George Sand to Gustave Flaubert

[Nohant, 14 September 1871]

What! You want me to stop loving? You want me to say I have been wrong all my life and that humanity is contemptible and despicable, always has been and always will be? You criticize me for the pain I feel as if it were some childish hankering after a lost illusion. What you say is that the people have always been uncivilized, that priests have always been hypocrites, the bourgeoisie always cowards, soldiers always brigands and that peasants have always been stupid. You say you have known this since your childhood, that you have never been in any doubt about it and that your mature years have therefore brought no disappointment. Have you never been young, then? How different we are. I have never stopped being young if loving is a characteristic of youth.

How do you think I could possibly isolate myself from my own kind, from my compatriots, from my race, from the great family of which mine is but one ear in this earthly wheatfield? As if it could possibly grow to ripen alone and as if we could live for a chosen few and separate ourselves from all the rest! The whole idea is impossible. Your strong desire to rationalize makes you in fact imagine the most unrealizable Utopia. In what garden of Eden, what fantastic Eldorado, could you hide your family, your little circle of friends and your own private happiness? How could you remain unaffected when the very fabric of society is torn to shreds by your own country's misfortunes? If your happiness resides in a select few, they themselves, the loved ones closest to your heart, must themselves by happy. Can they be so? Could you promise them any sort of security? Could you for example find refuge for me in old age, close to death? And what does either life or death mean to me now? I suppose that the whole of you dies and that love does not follow you into the other world. If so, how could you not feel till your dying breath the desire, the urgent need, to secure the greatest happiness for those you leave behind? Could you go peacefully to sleep feeling the earth shake, ready to engulf all those for whom you live? To live together as a family is no doubt a great good, comparatively speaking; it may well be the whole consolation one should hope to receive. But even if we suppose that evil from the outside could not make its way into our homes (and you know how impossible that is) I could still not bring myself to be part of what makes humanity miserable.

You could see all this coming, you say, and yes, of course I could see it as well as anyone else. I felt the gathering of the storm and like every other conscious person I sensed the coming of this cataclysm. But is it any consolation to know and recognize the sickness that makes the patient before you writhe in agony? When the storm of thunder breaks, are we any the calmer for having heard it growl in the distance? No, no, you cannot isolate yourself. You cannot break our ties of blood, you cannot vilify and condemn your own species. Humanity is not a meaningless word. Our lives are founded on love and to stop loving is to cease to live.

The populace, you say! You and I *are* the populace! You cannot get away from that; there are no two races;

inequalities arising from class distinctions are becoming relative or illusory. I do not know if your ancestors were from the upper middle classes but as for myself, on my mother's side, my roots go straight back to the people. I feel them live within me constantly.

Everyone's roots are there, in fact, however faded the memories have become. The first men were hunters and herdsmen; then they became farmers and soldiers and the first social distinctions were the result of successful plundering. There is probably not a single title that does not originate in some human bloodshed or other. We have to put up with whatever ancestry we may have, of course, but not even the most foolish among us could consider these first trophies of hatred and violence signs of glory to prevail over everything else. The *people* is always uncivilized, you say. I say the nobility has always been brutal.

There is no doubt that, along with the peasant, the aristocracy has been the class most resistant to progress and the least civilized in consequence. Any thinking person is proud not to belong to it. If we are from the bourgeoisie, if we are the descendants of the serf and the forced labourer, how could we bring ourselves to bow, in respect and love, to the sons of our fathers' oppressors? Those who deny the people vilify themselves . . . Bourgeoisie! If we want to lift our heads and become a class again, there is only one thing to do – we must proclaim ourselves to be the people and fight to the death against those who maintain superiority over us by divine right. We have not lived up to the dignity of the revolution. Because we aped the nobility, borrowed its titles and its trappings, and because we have been shamefully ridiculous and cowardly, we no longer count. We are nothing now and the people, with whom we should have been as one, denies us and seeks our destruction.

The populace uncivilized? No, nor is it stupid. Its present sickness is ignorance and folly . . . And what makes you believe that this proletariat, captive in Paris and numbering at most eighty thousand soldiers born of hunger and despair, represents the people of France? It does not even represent the people of Paris, unless you want to maintain the distinction I reject, between producer and trafficker? . . . I will press you even further and ask what the distinction you make is based on. Is it on more or less education? There are no boundaries here if you see the highest ranks of the bourgeoisie as scholars and literati and the lowest ranks of the populace as ignorant illiterates. You have to admit the many in between, some wise, intelligent members of the proletariat and some bourgeois with neither wisdom nor intelligence. The vast majority of our citizens were civilized yesterday. Many of those who can read and write have mothers and fathers alive who can barely sign their names.

Does the distinction rest on wealth? Would it be wealth alone that divides people into two separate camps? If so, you again have to ask yourself where the people begins and where it ends since wealth is shifted every day; one man is prostrated by financial ruin and another raised by fortune. The bourgeois of this morning may be a proletarian by evening and the proletarian of yesterday the bourgeois of today if he comes into money and a rich uncle dies. Names mean nothing and the business of classing, by whatever method, takes you round in circles.

People are only inferior and superior to each other according to how much reason and moral sense they possess. Education, if it merely develops the possibility of self indulgence, is no better than the ignorance of a proletarian who is honest through habit and instinct. Compulsory education which we all desire, from respect for human rights, is not a panacea; its miraculous powers must not be exaggerated. Those with wicked natures will find in it ever more ingenious and undetectable ways of doing harm. Like everything else that can be used or abused by people, education will be both the poison and the antidote.

The search for an infallible remedy for our ills is an illusion. We must all of us use, every day, those means immediately available to us . . . France is dying, that is certain, and we are all corrupt, ignorant and sick at heart. But to say all this was *ordained*, that it should be so, that it always has been and always will be, is simply to re-enact the fable about the drowning child and the teacher. You can say you do not care but you cannot add that it has nothing to do with you. The deluge is upon us and death approaches. It will do you no good to beat what you call a wise retreat. Your sanctuary will be invaded in its turn. And as you perish with human civilization, you will be no more sanguine for having ceased to love. Your philosophy will be no more sensible than that of people who throw themselves into the water in the hope of saving some shreds of humanity. If the shreds are not worth saving, so be it! They may go and we die with them, certainly, but we will pass into oblivion from the warmth of the living. I prefer that to an icy hibernation in anticipation of death. Besides, I could not act otherwise. Love does not reason. If I were to ask you why you have a passion for study, you could no more explain than the lazy can explain their sloth.

People of France, let us love each other! My God, let us love each other or we are lost! Let us reject, let us smother, let us crush the politics which divide us and lead us to take up arms against each other. Let us ask no one what they were and what they sought yesterday. Yesterday we were all in error. Let us know what we want today. And if it be not liberty for all and fraternity towards each other, let us not attempt to resolve the problems of humanity. We will be neither fit to define nor capable of understanding them.

The unleashing of the basest instincts, the frustration of ruthless ambition and the scandal of shameless usurpation of power, that is the dreadful spectacle that we have just witnessed. In the hearts of those politicians most devoted to democratic principles, this Commune has produced the most profound disgust . . .

And you, my friend, wish me to look on all this with stoical indifference? You want me to say man was ever thus, his nature foul and crime his means of expression? No, no, a hundred times no! Humanity is indignant with me and within me. This indignation is one of the passionate forms of love and we must neither suppress it nor forget it. We shall have to make immense efforts in brotherly love to repair the ravages of hatred. We must wipe out this plague, crush this infamy and bring about through faith the rebirth of our nation.

Two days later she added:

[Nohant, 17 September 1871]

Dear old boy,

I started to reply to you the day before yesterday but my letter became so long that I sent it as my next fortnight's piece for *Le Temps* – I've promised to let them have two a month. In this *Letter to a Friend*, you are not designated, even by initial, since I don't want to argue with you in public. In it I explain the reasons for my suffering and for my continuing to *will*. I shall send it to you and it will feel like talking to you again. You will see that my sorrow is part of me and that I cannot stop believing in progess. Without this hope, none of us is worth a thing. *Mandarins* do not need knowledge and the education of even a few of them has no validity unless it is in the hope of influencing the populace . . . I'm glad you liked the little pictures of the children. I embrace you very warmly; however much of a mandarin you pretend to be, you'll never be a Chinaman to me. I love you with all my heart. I'm working like a galley slave.

G. Sand

Such enormous differences notwithstanding, the friendship blossomed and in 1873, surrounded by friends and family, Sand invited Flaubert a second time to Nohant where they were joined by their mutual friend, Turgenev. It was a joyful time, with much clowning, dancing, singing and jollity. George Sand was by all accounts very good company; enthusiastic, funny and energetic. Her *auguste permanence* as she self-deprecatingly referred to her capacity for writing, was punctuated by periods of commensurately great relief and recreation.

Their correspondence continued virtually uninterrupted until Sand's death in 1876. Although Flaubert's opinion of her literary work varied, personal relations between them remained close and warm.

Flaubert to George Sand

[Sunday night 6 February] 1876

Chère maître, you must think me a *real* pig – I have not replied to your last letter and haven't yet said anything about the two latest volumes you sent me, let alone the third which arrived this morning.

For the last fortnight I have been entirely taken up with my little story* which will soon be finished. I have had so many things to contend with, various reviews to

St Julien, l'hospitalier.

send off and so forth but most importantly, my poor niece's health is giving grave cause for concern and I'm most worried. I don't know what I'm doing these days. A really bad patch. She's extremely anaemic, she's getting weaker and weaker and she has had to give up painting, which was her only distraction. None of the usual tonics seem to do anything for her. For the last few days, following the advice of a doctor I think a little more sound than the others, she has begun a course of hydrotherapy. I wonder if he will get her to digest and to sleep, to get up some strength. Your old Cruchard is less and less thrilled with existence as it proceeds, in fact he's had just about enough of it, infinitely too much, you might say. Much better to talk about your books.

I found them amusing and to prove it I must tell you I read *Flamarande* and *Deux Frères* one after the other without stopping . . . The reader's interest is held throughout, it increases apace in fact. What strikes me about these two novels, as indeed about all your work, is the natural progression of ideas, the talent you possess, the genius, rather, for narrative. But what an idiot that *Flamarande* of yours is and as for the servant telling the tale, who is obviously in love with his mistress, I wonder why you weren't more specific in showing his own personal jealousy.

Apart from the count, all the characters in your story are virtuous, extraordinarily so, I'd say. Do you really think they're true to life? Are there many people like that? While you're reading about them, you accept them because of the author's craftsmanship, but what about afterwards?

I think, *chère maître*, and this brings me to your last letter, that the great difference between us is this: in everything you do, you soar immediately up into the heavens and it is from there that you return to earth. You start with the ideal, with the theory. Hence your great

aptitude in life, your serenity, or to give it its proper
name, your greatness. I am the sort of poor ignoramus
that remains stuck to the earth, as bound to it as if I had
on soles of lead. Everything affects me, I am torn apart,
destroyed, and I try as hard as I possibly can to rise
above it. If I were to adopt your global perspective I
should become quite simply laughable. Preach at me
though you may, I cannot change my temperament, nor
the aesthetic that follows from it. You reproach me for
not letting myself go 'naturally'. Well, what happens to
discipline then? What about restraint? What are they for?
I admire Monsieur Buffon,* who put on handcuffs to
write. A little luxury full of symbolic meaning. What I
try and do, in my naïvety, is to be as understanding as
possible. And what more can you ask?

As for allowing my personal opinion of the characters
to intrude on the scene, no, no, no, a thousand times no!
I don't see one has any right to. If the readers don't find
in the book the message that's in it, then either they are
fools or the book is *false*, that's to say failing in accuracy.
As sure as something is true, it's good. Obscene books
are not immoral because they contain no truth. Things
don't happen like that in real life.

By the way, do please understand that I loathe what
people see fit to call *realism*. I'm supposed to be one of its
leading advocates and I wonder if you can possibly do
something about this.

As for the taste of the public, it never fails to amaze
me. Yesterday, for example, I went to the opening night
of *Prix Martin*, an amusing little farce that I personally
find full of wit. Not one line raised a laugh from the
audience and the dénouement, which is quite wonderful,

*1707–88. Renowned French naturalist who in his discourse 'On Style', on
admission to the Académie Française, coined the phrase '*le style est l'homme*'.
Flaubert's comment is a reference to Buffon's belief in self-discipline in
style.

went completely over their heads. So you could not be more mistaken if you try and please the public. I defy anyone to tell me how it's done. Success is a consequence; it should never be one's aim. I have never really sought it, even though I desire it and I do so less and less as time goes by.

After this little novella I shall write another.* I am too consumed by worry to start on a major work. I had thought of publishing *Saint Julien* in a periodical but I have decided against it for the time being . . .

'You will see,' wrote Flaubert, 'from my *Histoire d'un Coeur simple*', in which you will recognize your own direct influence, that I am not as stubborn as you think. I think the moral nature of it, or rather, the sympathy underlying this little work, will be pleasing to you.

In the last year of her life, George Sand wrote *Marianne*. It is the story of the emancipation of a young woman, and of her education, through action, of the man appointed as her guardian. He loves and is loved by her. Only gradually does this become apparent to them as her independence is both recognized and guaranteed and as his paternal role is relinquished. The simple revelation that Marianne thinks and feels much the same way as her godfather does leads them to greater happiness than either had been led by society to expect.

Set in her beloved Berry, to which George Sand was now virtually retired, it reflects the calm of her mature years. Marianne represents Sand's feminine ideal, the woman who achieves independence through honesty and who rejects the notion of marriage either as a form of insurance against loneliness and social opprobrium or as a reward for exclusive

Un Coeur simple.

proprietary rights.

There is much of both the young and the old George Sand in this tale: the inexperienced heiress unsure of the ways of the world, yet confident in the virtues of simplicity; the country girl at odds with the values of the city; the naturalist passionately interested in the flora and fauna of her native heath; the woman of wit and humour wary of the power of words. George Sand once said that her respect for the knowledge acquired intuitively by illiterates was equal in important ways to her respect for that housed in the ill-fated library of Alexandria. Marianne's admiration and humility with regard to what she termed the 'inarticulable' is similar to George Sand's view of 'the most eloquent of all languages – music'. Each expresses a profound mistrust of artistic values based on the dominance of form over content, technique over inspiration, and virtuosity over feeling.

The revolutionary Muse or 'Marianne' of the French Republic is here symbolized not by the largely martial images depicted in the *mairies* and on the stamps of France to this day, but by joint and equal partnership between man and woman in the setting of the home. Marianne's love for the wild garden and her affinity with untamed nature is the basis of her most intimate relationship with her world-weary and disillusioned future lover. The unaffected nature of life at Nohant, and her organic relationship to its maintenance and that of its family, was similarly the cornerstone of George Sand's social and political activity.

Appearing in conjunction with one other novella in 1876, *Marianne* was the last of George Sand's published works and forms a fitting literary conclusion to a life dominated, through its absence, by the question of marriage. By the time of its publication, Sand had lived through the horrors of the Franco-Prussian war and through the Paris Commune. As she grew older, she became increasingly less optimistic in her political beliefs and increasingly sickened by the bloodshed and violence accompanying every shift in power. The preoccupations of her life narrowed down to the circle of her immediate family and friends and she became known as *la Bonne Dame de Nohant*. With her husband, many lovers and many friends now long since dead, her friendship with Flaubert was a source of joy. Some months before her own death, she sent him a copy of her final publication. Of it, he wrote:

Flaubert to George Sand

[Friday night . . . 1876]

Thank you from the bottom of my heart, *chère maître*. Thanks to you I have just spent the most exquisite day. For I have only just read your last volume, *La Tour de Percemont* and *Marianne*. Since I had quite a lot to finish lately, *Saint Julien* amongst other things, I had put your stories away in a drawer so as not to be tempted. Having finished last night, the first thing I did this morning was rush to find them and devour them.

I thought they were two gems. Perfect. *Marianne* moved me deeply and two or three times I found myself weeping. I saw a lot of myself in Pierre and some pages could have been excerpts from my own memoirs, if I had talent enough to write like that. It's so charming and poetic and *true*. The *Tour de Percemont* I liked enormously but it was *Marianne* that literally enchanted me. I see that the English are of the same opinion. In the latest number of the *Athenaeum* there is a very good article on you, did you know? Anyway, this time I have not the slightest reservation. I am full of admiration.

You see how happy you have made me. But then you've never done me anything but good and I love you most tenderly. . . .

Marianne

I

What is it that you think about, Sleeping Beauty, as you ride along the country lanes on that skinny mare of yours? And not so much of a beauty either, come to think of it. Too skinny, too pale, too dull. Not a glimmer of sparkle in those big dark eyes. Still, I do wonder, when you're riding past the hedges, little dreaming you are watched, I wonder what exactly it is you go out for. What sort of things are going through your mind? You look straight ahead, far into the distance and I wonder, do your thoughts travel that far too, or do they stay close to home, wrapped up in yourself?

So ran the silent thoughts of Pierre André as he watched Marianne Chevreuse slow her horse to a walking pace. Passing under the walnut trees and reaching the river, horse and rider broke into a trot and, at a bend near some boulders, disappeared out of sight.

Marianne was a young country girl, now owner of a decent-sized *métairie** which brought in some 5,000 francs of revenue per annum. In local terms, this represented a capital of about two hundred thousand. Marianne was therefore a relatively good catch, yet at twenty-five years of age, she had still to find herself a husband. She was said to be 'difficult' and given to eccentricity, a characteristic which in the eyes of the local community was infinitely more dangerous than vice itself.

*Farm held on a sharecropping agreement

She was criticized for her love of solitude. No one could understand how, on the death of her parents when she was twenty-two, she had been able to refuse offers of a home from several members of the family in town, an uncle and an aunt, not to mention two or three cousins. These relatives would have liked to take her in *en pension* and launch her into a society of which she would very quickly have become a valued member.

La Faille-sur-Gouvre was a sizeable town with a population of some four thousand. The latter included some thirty or so middle-class families whose individual fortunes ranged from between a hundred to three hundred thousand francs. Taking into account the presence also of some very eligible and well-established civil servants, the town offered a promising collection of possible suitors. Any heiress, however particular in her tastes, should have found it easy to choose, from within its ranks, a suitable partner in marriage.

Marianne, however, had preferred to remain living alone in the country house her parents had left her. Occupying a secluded position surrounded by hills and woodland some four kilometres outside La Faille-sur-Gouvre, the house was in excellent condition and very adequately furnished within.

The region itself was near the centre of France, an unusually quiet area even by today's standards, and all the more so fifty years ago, when the events of this homely tale took place*. Never within living memory had any breath of scandal touched it. The peasants there are easy-going and regular in their habits. They generally own a little land and hold each other in mutual respect. Houses were few and far between in the area where Marianne and Pierre lived, since the great stretches of heathland, being unsuitable for small farming, were mostly owned by a few local bigwigs.

*i.e. *circa* 1825.

As the story begins, Pierre André was nearing forty. Only the year before, he had come back to live in the country, not far from the home of Marianne Chevreuse. He was in the process of restoring his own, more modest little house, with a view to spending the rest of his days there. The young woman, then, was about to embark on a life of solitary reflection, looking perhaps to the future for what the past had failed to bring. In contrast, the older and more mature Pierre, her godfather, friend and neighbour since childhood, in building this quiet retreat that so exactly matched his inner nature, hoped for nothing more than quiet oblivion.

Like everyone else, Pierre André had once had ambitions. He was intelligent and hardworking and in his youth felt capable of anything. His mother, proud of his early successes, had soon seen in him the stuff of greatness. Old man André, however, who was both poor and miserly, had only grudgingly allowed his son to go to Paris and study law. He had made him such a stingy allowance that the boy had lived in dire poverty. It had been a cruel and seemingly endless existence. He was a gifted conversationalist and had a great talent for writing. But he was crippled with shyness and, outside his own circle of friends, found it impossible to behave with any degree of spontaneity. He could certainly never hope for a career at the bar. The idea of becoming some pettifogging kind of solicitor was abhorrent to him and besides, he knew very well that his father would never give up a foot of his precious land to set up his son in practice. Even had his father been prepared to make such an heroic sacrifice, Pierre would never have agreed to it. He was not sufficiently confident of being able to provide for his parents' old age. So he read law for form's sake alone. At the same time, he dabbled in other subjects. He loved natural sciences and quickly mastered their basic principles. As he did so, he felt his mind opening up to the powers of analysis and understanding that were within him. He might have become a writer; he wrote a great deal but published nothing for fear of being considered mediocre. Eventually, he found a job as tutor to two young boys of a good family and was given the task of guiding them on their educational travels.

II

It had been his life's dream to travel. He was very successful with his pupils, finding ever more interesting ways to teach them both history and nature in the places they visited. They covered Europe and part of Africa together and were about to embark for America when news came of the father's serious illness. The boys' return was ordered. As a result of his illness the father was left an invalid; the sons were appointed directors of his banking firm and in consequence Pierre's functions ceased abruptly. He was about thirty-five years old at the time and had some ten thousand francs in savings. His parents urged him to buy land near them and return to the countryside. After just a few weeks he found the constraints to which he had earlier been used too irksome. His urge to travel was as strong as ever and he set off soon afterwards for Spain which he had yet to explore to the full. From there he went to Africa and, when his small resources were finally depleted, returned to Paris to look again for work. Luck was against him. All he could find were menial jobs in various administrative offices. He found he was having to resign himself to the depressing life he had led once before. He worked merely to keep himself alive and wondered constantly what was the use, if all he could look forward to was drabness, misery and exhaustion. The sudden death of his father after a gradual and almost imperceptible decline brought him once again to his mother's side and back to the lovely hills of the Gouvre.

There, his mother's fond illusions about her son were

rudely shattered. She learned that despite years of labour and exile, he had earned no capital whatsoever. She also learned that he was content to live on the most modest of incomes, provided it kept him out of debt. She blamed Paris, the government and society in general for being so blind to Pierre's obvious talents. He could never make her understand that in order to make one's mark in the world it is necessary to have patronage, protection or a certain boldness in which he was conspicuously lacking. Pierre's infectious gaiety and playful exterior hid an insurmountable obstacle to success: lack of self-confidence. His dashed hopes, he believed, would make him ridiculous in the eyes of others. From his friends he expected neither help nor consolation. They in turn were unaware that he suffered, so well did he conceal the fact. His natural stoicism and resolute cheerfulness made them think he must be happier far than they. He had, however, suffered greatly, not from material deprivation which he mentally dismissed but from the bleak and bitter isolation of a man with neither means nor connections.

Possessing every kind of artistic impulse, he could not make the leap from feeling to action, from inspiration to expression. He would like, for example, to have continued his interest in the theatre, but could not afford the expense; he loved painting and was an excellent judge of it but the daily grind of work crushed all else. He had a passionate interest in politics, but no base from which to develop his ideas and too much scepticism to become the mouthpiece of any party or leader.

Love he had experienced with painful intensity, and hopelessness too, since he always fell for superior beings far out of his reach. For months on end, for example, he had been in love with La Pasta.* Having seen her once or twice

*Giuditta Pasta, a celebrated Italian diva of the period

on the stage, he waited nightly for her shadowy figure to appear and disappear through the stage door. There had also been a certain Mademoiselle Mars,* the mere thought of whose eyes and voice had made him ill with longing. In his passion for these stars, he had forgotten to look at what lay closer to hand. When the chance of falling more reasonably in love occurred, he argued to himself that love and reason were incompatible. He therefore transferred all his feelings to his earlier love of nature and the beauty she has to offer. He was consumed with a desire to see at least the Pyrenees or the Alps once more. Sometimes he would go so far as to wonder whether he should not give up everything and become a tramp. What was the point of clean linen and a smart turnout when he could just as easily roam the world in rags, asking alms from time to time from total strangers? He yearned for a bohemian kind of life in which he would be free to wander into the farthest corners of the world, happy if hospitality were offered, equally content to sleep under a starry sky at night. Onward, towards ever changing horizons, that was the life! During these periods of utter dejection he would consider himself the feeblest of creatures, lacking in will-power, drive and conviction. He was nothing but a provincial hack, he thought, wild-eyed with rapture over the splendours of civilization and of nature yet afraid of his own shadow.

---

*A leading Comédie Française actress

III

Pierre felt humiliated by his lack of success in the eyes of the world and for not having been able to achieve his own independence. He returned to the fold to accept gladly the most immediate duty that befell him, that of comforting and supporting his mother in her old age. His only desire was to spare her the hardship and deprivation he himself had once endured. The old lady's needs in food and clothing were few enough but the dilapidated house which had been her home for fifty years was dangerous to her health. Pierre had it renovated and extended. This expense used up all the contents of a pouchful of écus Pierre had found in his father's desk.

The name of the house, possibly druidic in origin, was Dolmor. It was probably worth about 50,000 francs and the income from even such a limited amount of capital was in those days sufficient to keep a small country household in relative ease. They would eat meat twice a week; eggs and dairy produce came from the farm itself. A single manservant was enough if there was a horse to look after, since both mistress and farmer's wife would manage the house between them. Even one horse was a considerable luxury in those days. The farmer's brood mare would be taken to market when necessary and her fodder deducted from the farm expenses. Today, every self-respecting peasant has his own horse and trap but in 1825, the sight of a villager in possession of so much as an umbrella was very rare. Country women generally rode pillion to market behind either the farmer or the farm lad.

Indeed, Mademoiselle Chevreuse, richer of course than Pierre André, had scandalized the neighbourhood by insisting on riding alone. Her hunting saddle was the object of great curiosity to those she passed, yet her mount was very modest. It was a local-born filly that she herself had broken in at home and trained. It now recognized and followed her about like a dog. There had been loud protestations from the farmer when Mademoiselle Chevreuse had declared her intention of keeping it for herself and she had had to pay him half its price in order to do so. The whole farm had voiced alarm over the dangers to which the young mistress was exposing herself. And despite all the care and attention she lavished on the animal, Suzon remained a skinny little creature. By nature and temperament she was suited to her native heathland; tough and wiry she was also a smooth, clever little horse where the going was rough. She could be mischievous but never with malice. She knew no fear and although she was as gentle as could be with her mistress, she was no easy mount for anyone else.

Living alone as she did, Marianne needed some intelligent conversation every day, if only for an hour. Her parents had been on close terms with Pierre and she had remained very good friends with his mother. She went to see her every night to play draughts and chat till the old lady's bedtime around nine o'clock at the latest. The ride home alone for Marianne took only a few minutes. Suzon galloped it in one go, never putting a foot wrong, even on the darkest nights.

Pierre had known Marianne practically since the cradle. As a gangling schoolboy home on holiday he had seen her learning to walk and carried her about in his arms or on piggy-back. As the years went by, she grew bigger and taller and they remained close friends. But as his visits home became rarer, he found on his return that his little neighbour's early promise of beauty remained unfulfilled. He was convinced she must be suffering from some wasting disease and showed the most tender solicitude towards her. In the end he had disappeared for five whole years. When he came back, to settle down for good at Dolmor, he found his god-daughter at his mother's side, comforting her as best she could and helping her to while away the time until his long-awaited return.

Afterwards, Marianne changed her routine and no longer came of an evening to entertain her old neighbour and see to her needs. She chose days when Pierre was away or when some job or other took him from the house. Then she would come and keep Madame André company as before.

This had been the situation for almost a year, during which Pierre had scarcely paid attention to Marianne. His mind, after his return home, was weighed down with two equally heavy burdens: a disillusioned past and a future without prospects. He did not believe that his life, hitherto unblessed by happiness, was likely to improve in the future. It was better to snuff out once and for all every vestige of hope left in his heart. He had resolved to submit to fate, to fight no longer against the impossible and to keep his spirits as calm as his nature. The most he could hope for was to take care of his own needs as far as possible, to be comfortable at least, and thankful that the fear of dying cold, weak and hungry in some distant garret or hospital was now forever removed.

Despite all this, Pierre André had for some days now been

prey to a strange, feverish excitement. The little house and garden which had hitherto absorbed all his energies were nearly completed. Furthermore, he had received a letter which had for some strange reason filled him with deep unease.

IV

The letter was from a Monsieur Jean Gaucher, a tradesman formerly of La Faille-sur-Gouvre who had left the town ten years previously and now ran a successful business in Paris. It read:

My dear André,

I have a great favour to ask you which will probably take up no more than five minutes of your time. It is about my son Philippe, who is much more of a lightweight than his brother, and much less of a scholar. He claims to want to go in for the arts, if you please, and take up the profession of painter. He is a boy of some intelligence and has a good heart. However, he is totally lacking in good judgement and has no thought at all for the future. You must remember him yourself and despite all his faults you would still consider yourself his friend, I trust. We need your help in marrying him off. I have spent a great deal of money on him but so far, he himself has not earned a single sou. I should be a fool if I imagined things would change in the future. However, I can set him up with one hundred thousand francs; he is a kind-hearted, good-looking fellow and our family name is beyond all reproach. So I think he might aim for a bride in the two-hundred thousand mark. Then, instead of working, he could set to and paint, since this is his obvious preference. The only difficulty is finding a girl whose own needs would be modest enough to accommodate his. The chances of finding one here in Paris are remote. Back home, however, the good old

country ways still produce that kind of woman. I have my
eye on the Chevreuse girl. She is in a good financial
position and country-bred. I knew her parents, decent
folk, and last year I caught a glimpse of the girl herself at
La Faille. She is no beauty but you could not call her
hideous either. In your last letter, you yourself were
telling us how good she had been to your mother. Since
she is as yet unmarried, I think my son will be a suitable
match for her.

Therefore, dear friend, I am sending Philippe to stay
with you for a week. He will arrive on the 7th of this
month. He himself is not averse to marriage but he will
need a woman who looks good and knows how to behave.
Presumably he will be able to have a look at Marianne
Chevreuse while he is with you. If she is to his liking,
feel free to conclude the business there and then or, if
you prefer, after he has returned here.

I count on you as a dear friend of long standing and
hope that in, similar circumstances, you would do
likewise.

There was a twofold reason why this blunt, but nevertheless
straightforward letter should give rise to intense irritation in
Pierre André's breast. Firstly, he considered Jean Gaucher
cavalier in his manner towards him. Gaucher had always
been relatively wealthy yet Pierre, even in times of direst
need had never considered their friendship close enough to
ask for his help in any way. Though Gaucher had known how
few resources were at Pierre's disposal, he had always been
far too hardheaded a businessman to dream of offering him
employment. Pierre was too well educated; Pierre was too
distinguished; Pierre must, or so Gaucher affected to
believe, set himself considerably higher sights.

Pierre therefore felt himself under no obligation whatsoever. He considered it the height of rudeness to send to his

home a stranger who would more than likely neither thank him for his hospitality nor offer intellectual compensation for Pierre's wasted time. He had very slight acquaintance with the young man. He called him *tu* for he had known him since his childhood, but felt no warmth towards the boy. In fact Pierre had always found Philippe altogether too self-assured for his age. Besides, he had not seen him for nearly four years. He knew too little about him to feel confident in supporting his suit to any girl, let alone to Marianne. Pierre respected her as an irreproachable person to whom he was bound by ties of natural affection, of gratitude and still more, by his responsibility as her godfather.

His first instinct was therefore to write as follows:

> My dear Gaucher,
>   I fear I am singularly ill-suited for the mission with which you seek to entrust me. Having no personal experience in the delicate business of marriage, I am the least well-qualified to help anyone else in such an undertaking. Besides, your plan seems to me a little fanciful. You may remember that Mademoiselle Chevreuse is twenty-five years old. More than likely, she will find Philippe too young a suitor and I am not certain whether or not she has decided to give up her own liberty. To ask her opinion in such matters would seem to me an indiscretion to which my years do not as yet entitle me . . .

You old fool! cried Pierre to himself, stopping abruptly there. What will that achieve? Gaucher's scorn, that's all! He's sixty years old and thinks everybody else is too. And besides, what you're saying isn't true! Why should you not speak of love to your god-daughter? How could she ever take offence at your efforts to secure her happiness? Her firm and unblushing response might well be to receive the suitor in question. Furthermore, if she were to learn later that you had contrived his removal, what might she think of you? . . . No I cannot send this letter! I shall write that, since I am called away, I shall have to ask the Gauchers to find a different representative.

V

Pierre André tore up the letter. As he was about to begin a second, he realized that no post would leave La Faille-sur-Gouvre till the following day, that it would take two days to reach Paris and that no letter from him would be delivered till the very day, perhaps the very hour of Philippe's departure. It was therefore already too late to refuse and Monsieur Jean Gaucher must already be relying upon his compliance.

He resigned himself to events and went down to the river, thinking to soothe his vexation by a walk through the lovely meadows that surround its clear waters. It was at this spot that, many a time before, he had seen Marianne pass by and given no heed to her at all. Now, however, hidden by the willows and the entwined branches of white bindweed and wild balsamine, the sight of her moved him disturbingly. Instead of calling out his usual cheerful greeting, he plunged deeper into the branches and began to reflect somewhat bitterly on the ironic turn of recent events.

His thoughts formed the opening monologue of our tale. Writing was, as we have seen, one of his chief pleasures. He had committed his thoughts to paper, since he had even felt a certain vocation for it. Great outbursts of feeling within him had remained somehow incomplete until expressed in words. The intensity of these feelings had dominated his life hitherto and drained his emotions completely. He had until now constantly pushed them aside, never trying to translate them. Today, however, he decided that the feelings which normally overwhelmed him would be dominated only if he succeeded in subjecting them to careful analysis.

He always had on him a fairly large notebook in which he often wrote during his morning walk. Deeply interested as he was in natural history, in painting and in archaeology, he often jotted down some comment or other or dashed off a quick sketch of a ruin or piece of landscape. Since both art and nature were pleasures he allowed himself to savour and enjoy, he often found that his observations upon them took a somewhat literary turn.

'What I must guard against is daydreaming,' he said to himself. 'Lost in my own imagination I evaporate like mist in the sun. When I manage to express my delight in things, I am happy. So why should the same not apply to suffering, if I were to try and express it today? For I am indeed suffering, the devil knows why. And I could continue to do so for a very long time to come without ever discovering the reason why. Out of the clouds! Consciousness emerge! Let us see things for what they are! If I can formulate something then it must exist. If it turns out to be nothing, it will disappear!' Musing thus, Pierre sharpened his pencil, opened his notebook and, sitting on the grass in the shade of the willows and the alder, wrote as follows:

VI

My little retreat is nothing like the idyllic dream I once had of
it and I must confess that for over a week I have been most
excruciatingly bored. I should like the place to be moss-clad
and covered with vines and clematis but until everything I
have planted has had time to cover them, all I shall be able
to see are blank white walls and brand-new brickwork.
Fortunately, my mother loves it all and promises to live to a
hundred in what she calls a palace. Well, long may the poor
dear woman live there and much pride and happiness may it
bring her. As for myself I shall just have to learn to accept the
unutterable tedium which will probably be my lot as long as I
live here. I say probably, but who knows? For a long time I
used to think that with so much capacity for regret and for
hope within me, I should, if it came to it, find I had an equal
capacity for calm resignation. But either my mental balance
is destroyed or it has yet to be established. I wonder, am I too
young or too old? Am I a broken man or am I simply worn
out? And what difference does it make in the end? More than
likely I am a man consumed. Wild beasts have devoured the
half of me and what is left of my faint heart beats only to
remind me of what is lost. Vain and useless lamentations!
And who could possibly care? My mother is unaware of my
misery and who else but she could share the pain?

Marianne? What about Marianne? I think of her since
she's the only person save my mother who is part of my
private life. But there is too great a distance between us for

me to include her in my thoughts; too great a difference in age, in experience and in mentality.

She does seem to think a great deal, it's true, but she's so quiet. She never seems to need to unburden herself of her thoughts. I think she must be very happy. She has such a remarkably equable character. And as for her health, which used to be so delicate and gave us such cause for concern over the years, she seems now to have developed a cast-iron constitution. Cold, heat, rain, snow, nothing seems to affect her. Not even when she spends hours on horseback or caring for the sick. She has spent countless nights nursing various invalids, my father in particular, and when my mother was exhausted, Marianne was always awake and quite indefatigable. She cannot be very sensitive, for she did not weep at my mother's tears. And yet she was always at her side and always managed to take her mind off her worries. There is no doubt she is a good, generous, brave and loyal woman. If I were ten years younger and a hundred thousand francs richer, I should most certainly have aspired to making her my life's companion. I should be very surprised if she inspired love in me but there could have been a kind of high regard and boundless trust in each other which might have made me happy. What am I saying? I could never be happy under such conditions! Once having experienced the joy of love, its anguish and its burning pain, one can never be satisfied with a peaceful stable relationship, however good, however attractive that might seem. Love is a madness, a wild dream that carries one into impossible realms. How could one impose such a thing on a decent honest creature who deserves better? But possibly I overestimate Marianne's capacity to feel suffering. Would she be troubled at all, one wonders, by either dearth or excess of feeling? Certainly, if she were capable of love, which is unlikely. Between the ages of fifteen and twenty-five, a woman's life is subject to wild fluctuations of the emotions and of the imagination. Marianne has weathered this with perfect equanimity. Hers is a strong, cold little soul I fear. Having come through that crisis, she is like a rock. Our stolid peasant ways have imposed themselves upon her, as they will make me, too, impassive before too long, I hope. To think I may have another ten years before all the fire has gone out of me! Suppose I were to ask Marianne the secret of her dubious success? She would not understand me. She could not answer me. She would find it stupid of me not to understand her. I would have to confess, it *is* stupid, but I have no idea what she is like. The fact is, of course, that very few men are capable of understanding or really knowing women. Generally speaking, those who fascinate us and resist us remain mysteries to us. Those who give themselves to us lose all prestige and after our senses have drunk to the full of them, we cease to follow the movements of their souls. In this respect, marriage is a tomb. I congratulate myself on being too old and too poverty-stricken to get embroiled in it.

I have written nothing but nonsense for the past quarter hour. I read it over without understanding a thing. All I see is this ridiculous curiosity about Marianne. Here I am, worried and anxious; there she is, serenity incarnate. How can she appear before me like a human reproach? Like an ironic comment on my own life. How can she never suspect I might be miserable? Unlike myself, she is not protected by a mature, philosophical outlook on existence. Compared to me she is a child. No struggle has tested her strength, no disappointment has yet caused her spirit to waver. But that's it, by God! That's the very reason she is the stronger. She has lost nothing of herself. She has not been devoured by vultures and wolves! She is untouched. She lives life to the full. However feeble the flame within her it is enough to light her way. But as for me, the fire in my heart burns me alive.

VII

Pierre closed his notebook and put it in his pocket. He stayed for a while looking at the dragonflies chasing each other above the shimmering waters of the stream. He saw how their beautiful wings matched the iridescence of the flowing waters and compared the movements of the little waves with the gracefulness of their darting flight. He opened his notebook again and jotted down a few pretty phrases calling the dragonflies 'river nymphs' and 'hearts of flowers'. Then shrugging his shoulders in resignation he crossed out these lines and continued his journey to Dolmor. Although his walk had been without pleasure or profit, he thought to himself, at least he was free to go where he pleased in his own good time. And that, he mused, was better than dragging his weary feet through the dust and the smells of Paris to a meaningless job. During those days, as he had crossed the threshold of some dreary office or sleazy bar, he could remember with painful clarity thinking: Oh for a tree on the banks of the Gouvre and leisure to look into its clear waters. Little enough to ask for; too much, it would seem, to be granted.

What an ungrateful wretch I am, he said to himself. I have all I could wish for and still I am not happy. He came to the fork near the rocks and continued, eyes fixed to the ground, intent on some minor drama of nature, a fly, a blade of grass. He thought how lucky he was to light on such poetry here among the sandy paths of arrow broom and pink heather; what a contrast with the dirt and the filth of city streets. His thoughts flew to high mountains, to diamonds of snow under sun, to crests of blue ice beneath a sky of rose. Suddenly, thinking he had reached home, he drew up with a start. His mistake near the rocks became apparent as he found himself standing at the gates of Marianne's domain, Validat.

By the local standards of the day, Validat was a well-maintained *métairie*, yet a wet and smelly dunghill stood in a stagnant pool right in the middle of the yard. The yard itself was full of animals. It was just before the reaping season, when the oxen are not working but not yet out to pasture. To give the poor beasts somewhere to roam they are put into a kind of hedged enclosure. The gate to this was closed by a simple crown of interwoven branches. This was lifted over the first two bars of the gate and hooked round a large nail from a cart. The nail itself was buried into the trunk of an old tree that served as a gatepost. Once the crown is lifted, the long heavy gate swings open on hinges fixed to another tree or a log. The hedge itself is on a sloping bank topped with branches of dried hawthorn and layers of beaten earth. The enclosure hedge at Validat was very old and very beautiful. Its hedge held all the plants occurring naturally in its rich soil, blackthorn and hawthorn, elder, bramble, large branches of oak with one long side branch curved and interlaced with others, garlanded all round with hopvine and Virginia creeper. Its sloping banks were covered with velvety moss while speedwell and arrowhead grew along its little ditch, green with watercress.

Realizing his mistake and thinking he had no business important enough to disturb Marianne with, Pierre left the gate without lifting the crown of hawthorn. He told himself he was an idiot and made to retrace his steps.

Normally in a farm such as Validat, the landowner's quarters, consisting of a single ground-floor apartment, look out on to the farm itself, dunghill included, so that he can survey at his leisure the livestock in the yard and any business being done within its confines. Marianne had changed the whole arrangement. She had blocked up some windows and kept a single door between her and the rest of the household. On the opposite side of the building she had had windows let in and one set of french windows built. At ground level this side of the house looked out on what was once a sombre wall, now enlivened by a huge yellow jasmine. Hollyhocks of every colour towered over a fragrant clematis that grew in a thousand dense festoons. Here, too, she had had some four square metres of the ground paved to form a verandah. Surrounded by bushes and flowers, it had a tiled roof, to protect it from the damp. There was a path leading from it to the bottom of Marianne's garden. This in turn was small but charming. No grander than that of any of her peasant neighbours', it contained one or two vegetable patches, some pinks and some roses, and borders of lavender and thyme. In one corner grew the box tree from which they gathered branches on Palm Sunday and beyond this was an orchard. Its boughs hung over a fine lawn and encircling all was the traditional open wattle fence made, like that of the enclosure, of dried hawthorn branches.

It was in this isolated garden that Marianne Chevreuse read or did her needlework when she was not busy on the farm. She happened to be walking along her side of the old hedge just as Pierre André was walking along the sunken path outside which led to his own homestead. As their eyes met, each was surprised. They exchanged a warm but slightly uncomfortable greeting. Pierre, not understanding Marianne's unease, put it down to his own awkwardness of manner in bidding her good-day.

VIII

She asked him for news of his mother.

'She is well,' replied André, 'except that she misses you. You know you're getting to be quite a stranger these days! No sign of life from our little neighbour for over a week!'

'You haven't been away for a week, have you?'

'No, no, no, I've finished running about getting things for the garden and the house, that's all. Everything's finished and from now on I shall become my mother's constant and faithful companion. But does that mean we shall be deprived of your company?'

'It would be no great deprivation for you, I'm sure! However, if Madame André is lonely, tell her I shall come whenever she calls for me.'

'Oh, but you must come to her, my child. My mother cannot go much further than the garden now. She can't call for you any more and she would be so sad if you were to abandon her.'

'I have no intention of abandoning her. I simply imagine she would much rather be with you than with me and I could be in your way if I were to come to your house too often.'

'In our way? The very idea! Aren't you one of the family?'

And as Marianne remained silent, André, making a sudden effort to unburden himself of his secret anguish, declared:

'Marianne, you've become very strange. There are things about you I don't understand. May I speak freely? Do you have time to listen and give me an answer?'

'Yes, I have, I'm listening.'

'It's not easy, shouting at each other through this hedge, couldn't I come in?'

'I'll meet you at the stile.'

Marianne ran on ahead and arrived first. Skilfully lifting the great prickly hawthorn crown, she jumped nimbly over the stile and landed on the green path where André found her ready to listen to what he had to say.

'So we're not allowed in, it seems,' he said. 'I thought you might do me the honours of your garden.'

'My garden is not worth looking at, even though I do love it. You have such good taste, you would laugh at it and that would distress me.'

'When I say you're strange . . .'

'What makes you think that? You've never said anything like this before.'

'Well, first of all, why are you so formal with me since I came back for good. Is it out of respect for my great age?'

'You're not so old. And besides, I'm not all that young either.'

'Well, what is it then? Why don't you ever give a straight answer to a question?'

Marianne seemed surprised and, looking carefully at André, said:

'Are you in a bad mood today?'

He was struck by her composure and by the directness of her gaze. She had never looked at him like this before.

'It's true, I am in a bad mood,' he replied. 'I have something embarrassing to tell you and you're not helping me at all.'

'Embarrassing?' said Marianne, looking at him again, this time a little anxiously. 'What could there be embarrassing between you and me?'

'You'll soon find out. Let's walk for a bit. It's still a little too chilly to stay in the shade when we're warm. Will you give me your arm?'

'Well,' he said brusquely, as they began to walk on, 'here's the thing. A person who would like to make your acquaintance has approached me. I'm not sure that I can introduce him to you until I have your permission to do so. I do not want you to meet this person unprepared, as it were.'

'Thank you for that. You're quite right. I should hate a surprise. No doubt it has to do with marriage.'

'Precisely.'

'You know I have refused several offers?'

'So my mother mentioned. She says you do not want to be married, is that right?'

'No, that's not it. I just don't want any of the suitors that have come forward so far, that's all.'

'Were they not nice?'

'No, but I didn't like any of them enough.'

'Do you want to love your husband?'

'Naturally. The man you suggest . . .'

'I'm not suggesting anyone. I'm just acting on someone's behalf, that's all.'

'But without enthusiasm?'

'You're perfectly at liberty to send me packing but you must not refuse to listen to me. So far, you only know this person by name.'

'In that case, this is my answer: I shan't refuse to see him unless you tell me beforehand that he is not at all suitable.'

'Would you take my word for it?'

'You'd never deceive me.'

'Of course not, but . . . well the young man has one great fault, he's too young.'

'Younger than I?'

'Yes.'

'And?'

'And? and? What's the matter with you? You're dismissing the main objection.'

'I haven't said I'm not taking it into consideration. But I want to know a great deal more.'

'For the moment, he is less wealthy than you but later on he will probably be the richer.'

'Yes? What else?'

'What else? Nothing that I know of. I hardly know him except by sight. I've had very little talk with him.'

'What does he look like?'

'Quite handsome. Tall. Well built. Good-looking lad.'

'What sort of manner?'

'Self-satisfied. Smug, I'd say.'

'You haven't said a word about his family.'

'Very respectable. Well established. Local. Moved away about ten years ago.'

'You don't mean one of the Gaucher boys, do you?'

'I hadn't reckoned on telling you who it was until I had your permission to introduce him, but since you've guessed . . .'

'I don't remember them very well,' said Marianne thoughtfully. 'There are two or three of them, aren't there?'

'Two. It's the younger one who seeks your hand.'

'Seeks my hand! I've only got a dim recollection of him but he's only a child isn't he? He can't remember me at all. He must be after my little heap of capital.'

'Not exactly . . . but his father . . . Look here, I've got the letter on me. Since you know everything else, you may as well read it.'

Marianne stopped to read the letter from Gaucher *père*. She did so with her customary calm. André watched her expression. She smiled almost imperceptibly when she came to the two or three passages where the businessman put the question of the marriage in the crudest and most basic terms. To Pierre's surprise, she showed no annoyance and handing the letter back to him said:

'Well, let him come and we'll see.'

For a moment, Pierre felt strangely annoyed. Then returning to his usual bantering tone, he said:

'I see my mother was much mistaken. You *are* afraid after all, of turning into an old maid.'

'I must marry now or never,' replied Marianne. 'Later on, I should probably decide against it.'

'Why?'

'Because freedom is altogether too sweet and precious. If you get too accustomed to it, you miss it too much.'

'I quite agree with you. Marry then, since you still want to. I may expect Monsieur Philippe Gaucher as a guest very soon and I hope I will not have to show him the door on your behalf. He will be with us on Sunday morning. Come and have dinner with us that evening, do.'

'No, indeed. I don't think it would be proper for me to come to him. You bring Madame André over and have dinner with me instead, all three of you.'

'But you know she hardly goes anywhere now. How would she get back that night?'

'There's no difficulty there. I've bought an old rattletrap of a cart. We'll harness the farmer's big mare to it. Your mother's been promising me for a long time to come and have dinner with me when I found some form of transport for her.'

'So we will be admitted into the *sanctum sanctorum* to which you refused me entry earlier on?'

'Of course. Madame André will be with you.'

'So *I* am a stranger am I? Just another man, how odd!'

'It's not odd at all. When my parents were alive you used to be able to come and go as freely as you liked. But five years have passed since you last appeared in these parts. I have become an orphan in the meantime and must act circumspectly if I want to keep my reputation. You know how inquisitive and fond of gossip people are around here. We may live in the most isolated back of beyond but I could never receive a gentleman twice without there being plenty of talk in the neighbourhood.'

'What, from an old fellow like me, your godfather, your surrogate papa?'

'People would talk just the same. I know the locals, you've forgotten.'

'In that case, I will have to hope for your marriage. Simply so as to have the pleasure of your company more often.'

'I should not have thought it was such a pleasure for you, to be sure.'

'If you did, would you have deprived me of it so much?'

'Many's the time you have done without it quite voluntarily, as I remember.'

'It's true that I have often made use of the fact that you were there with my mother in order to do some work in my room. It was not very polite of me but I didn't think you would notice.'

'I was glad you felt free enough to rely on my devotion to her.'

'Glad! I should have much preferred it had you felt annoyed – or sorry, at least.'

'I beg your pardon?' Marianne drew herself up again and looked at André, her large dark eyes innocently questioning. The dominant expression in her face was astonishment. She looked as though she were waiting to have something explained, so as not to have to keep on guessing.

It seems, said André to himself, that I've just said something stupid. I cannot explain it. He was obliged to withdraw and thereby bring the conversation to a close.

'I mustn't tire you any further,' he said, letting Marianne's arm go. 'I forgot that the closer I get to my home, the further away you are from yours. Now that everything's settled, I have nothing more to ask you. I shall bring your fiancé to you on Sunday next.'

'I have no fiancé as yet,' replied Marianne coldly, 'and as for the Sunday plans, we shall have to see whether your mother is agreeable to being of the party. If not, I'm afraid the dinner will not take place. I shall come and invite her tonight, unless that's inconvenient.'

'No, not inconvenient at all,' said André, a little drily, annoyed and truly hurt by her formal little tone. 'Until later then!'

And sad and vexed, he continued on his way.

What a cold little creature she is, he said to himself as he walked briskly on. Narrow-minded, self-centred and ice-cold. Afraid of gossip, too, what a prude! What was I thinking of earlier when I was agonizing over what might be at the bottom of that peaceful lake. There is no bottom at all. And she's no lake either. She's nothing but a pond and full of rushes and frogs at that. That's what living in the country does to us! She used to be a sweet child, a perky, thoughtful little look about her, but now she's a strong girl; strong and calculating. A dry, self-disciplined little spinster.

IX

What do I care, he said to himself again as he arrived at the threshold of his home. This place of mine is perfectly fine; I did it less than justice this morning. Those stark white walls take on a tinge of pink when the sun hits them from this angle; my climbers have got some fine shoots coming up and by the autumn they'll have reached as far as the balcony. It's wonderful to have a home that's really one's own and to have perfect, unlimited freedom in which to enjoy it. I really shouldn't criticize my god-daughter for thinking of herself when I do exactly the same. Let's take life as it comes, the two of us!

'Come along, son,' called Madame André from the dining room. 'It's half-past five and your soup's getting cold!'

'And I've kept you waiting,' said Pierre, setting down his bagful of plants and stones. 'I didn't realize it was so late!'

He went quickly to the table after washing his hands at the little blue porcelain washbasin in the dining room. Over dinner, he warned his mother of Marianne's impending visit and the reason for it.

Madame André listened calmly to him until he told her how receptive Marianne had been to the idea of meeting Philippe Gaucher. She was incredulous.

'You're teasing me,' she said, 'or else Marianne is teasing you. Marianne does not want to marry. She's told me so a hundred times.'

'Well, she's forgotten then, because now she's saying the exact opposite. La donna e mobile! but what's the matter, mother, dear. You're not crying?'

'Perhaps I am. I don't know,' the good woman replied, wiping away with her napkin tears that were now streaming down her cheeks. 'My heart is very heavy. It wouldn't take much to make me weep.'

'Well, let's change the subject quickly then. We mustn't spoil your dinner. Look, mamma, you're very attached to Marianne, I know that; I also know that she is worthy of your friendship. Yet she's not so different from every other girl as she sometimes seems. Like all the others, she's been dreaming all this time about love and marriage. You could hardly expect her to give that up just to keep you company. She can't go on picking up your dropped stitches till kingdom come. She must think of herself, too. And good luck to her, I say.'

'Do you really think it's myself I'm feeling sorry for? Perhaps you're right after all! Yes, of course you are! Whatever happens I mustn't let her see how I feel. She's probably on her way by now. She must find me as gay and cheerful as you yourself must try to be.'

'I?' said André, surprised at the look his mother was giving him. 'And why should I be anything else, pray?'

'No reason. I just thought . . .'

'You have never, I hope, imagined *I* could be in love with Marianne, have you?'

'And what if you were? I for one wouldn't be sorry!'

'Mother, admit it, you've always dreamed of marrying me off to your dear little neighbour. How is it you haven't said a word about it to me?'

'I most certainly have! I've said several words about it in fact, but you were never listening.'

'When was that? I swear I don't remember.'

'Well, it's a long time ago now. Six years. It was on your

last trip home before your poor father died. You had some money at the time. We wanted you to marry so that you would stay near us. Marianne was twenty at the time; and she wasn't an orphan, independent and wealthy as she is now. You could have married her then.'

'And now I can't?' burst in Pierre, overcome with emotion. 'I am older and poorer than I was then. I wouldn't be suitable for her now! Dear mamma, I beg of you, never subject me to the humiliation of being refused by that disdainful, calculating little person! Don't speak to her of me, I implore you. I fervently hope you have not already done so!'

'Certainly I have, from time to time.'

'And what did she say?'

'Never a word. Marianne never answers when it could commit her.'

'That's true, I've noticed that. She's so distant. I find something repulsive about that. In a beautiful woman of the world, who knows from experience that the best way to attract admirers is to appear ice-cool, it might be understandable. But in a young country lass, seeking true love, there's something . . .'

'Hush! Here she comes,' said Madame André, greatly disturbed by her son's obvious and bitter disappointment. 'Let's not show how we really feel!'

X

They finished dinner and, at the sound of Suzon's steady trot, went out to meet Marianne. Hardly touching the reins, she jumped down as the gentle horse came to a halt. Following her at walking pace, Suzon turned to the left and went on by herself to find her habitual stall, a little corner of the barn that she knew of old and which she shared, on these occasions, with the farmer's old donkey.

Marianne's riding-costume was a simple dimity bodice, a round straw hat, and a long blue and grey striped skirt which she hitched up elegantly at the side to a thin leather belt. She wore her curly hair short and this girlish appearance, coupled with her slight figure, made her look about fourteen or fifteen at the most. Her flawless complexion had a slight, even tan about the eyes and the nape of the neck only. Her features were very delicate and her teeth very beautiful. All she needed to be really pretty was to believe herself so.

'Well now,' said Madame André, embracing her. 'We know what's brought our little darling to us tonight. So you've decided to get married!'

'No, Madame André,' replied Marianne, 'I have decided nothing, yet.'

'Ah, but, . . . since you've decided to receive a suitor, it follows you'll accept him if he suits you.'

'Well, that's the whole question. For the moment, I'm just looking, as they say. Are you willing to bring him over to me on Sunday?'

'Certainly, my dear, I could never refuse you anything.'

'I'll leave you two in peace to discuss this weighty problem,' said Pierre André, making for the meadow. 'On this
interesting topic, women always have little secrets they want
to confide in each other. I should be in your way.'

'Oh, no,' said Marianne. 'There are absolutely no secrets
between us and I refuse to think about the idea until both you
and your mother have told me what I should do about this
person.'

'What! You mean you would listen to what we thought
before you decided?'

'Certainly.'

'I cannot accept any such responsibility,' replied André
drily. 'I'm no connoisseur of husbands and I think you're
making fun of us, playing the innocent like this.'

'How could I be anything but innocent?' said Marianne,
her eyes opening wide in astonishment.

'Well, you know why you rejected the others so you must
know what you want and why you might accept this one!'

'Him, or someone else!' replied Marianne smiling. 'Don't
go away, please. I've got something to ask you.'

'Oh, *really!* That's too much! Now you want to know what
sort of husband you should choose, do you?'

The three sat down on a bench, with Madame André in the
middle.

'No,' replied Marianne. 'You couldn't tell me that. You
couldn't give me a serious answer because you're not very
interested in my future. No, I'd like to ask you something
which is only indirectly related to the question of marriage. I
should like to know whether a girl in my position can educate
herself without leaving her home and her accustomed ways.'

'What a very singular question she's putting to me,' said
Pierre to his mother. 'Can you make head or tail of it?'

'But of course I can,' replied Madame André. 'And this

isn't the first time Marianne has racked her brains over the problem. I am in no position to give her advice myself. All I've learned is what I was taught as a young girl. That is all that's necessary for a poor country housewife like myself. But it doesn't take you very far. There are many topics I never bring up because I don't understand the first thing about them. The wisest thing a woman in my situation can do is not to ask questions for fear of showing her own ignorance. But that's not good enough for Marianne. She doesn't want simply to learn tact and diplomacy; she would like to be able to talk about all sorts of things with educated people.'

'Forgive me, Madame André,' said Marianne, 'but I should like to be educated not so much for others' pleasure as for my own. I see for example that my godfather is happy walking about alone for days on end, thinking about all he knows. I'd like to know if he is happier than I, who go for the same long walks but without knowing anything and without thinking about anything.'

'Good heavens,' cried Pierre in surprise. 'You've just put your finger on the very thing that troubles me myself. What exactly is the secret mystery of unconscious life?'

'What? You've been pondering over whether there is anything inside my brain?'

'My God, I didn't mean you personally, dear child, but I've asked myself a thousand times the very question you've just put to me. When I see the deeply thoughtful look on some peasant face, when I see the exuberant joy in some children, when I see the apparently rapturous happiness of small birds and the blissful peace of flowers in the moonlight, I often ask myself if having a scientific explanation of the world is an advantage or not. Does the effort of reflection remove from unconscious mental activity its greatest charm? And does it remove from sensation its greatest power? I'm sorry if I sound pedantic, my way of putting things must seem ridiculous to you, but to be brief, I swear I have yet to find the answer. I count on you to enlighten me if you'd care to think one day about things other than the laundry or the market price of chickens.'

'I can only speak about what I know. I don't have words for all I think. I need time to find them. Will you wait while I try?'

XI

All three remained silent for a few moments. Marianne
looked as though she was trying to add up in her head a series
of large figures. Madame André seemed unsurprised by
Marianne's hesitant approach to formal argument. Only
Pierre was inwardly impatient. He seemed to have taken very
seriously the problem of resolving in his own mind that
morning's question, namely: was Marianne's intelligence
inexistent or merely dormant?

Eventually, with a hint of exasperation in her voice, she
broke the silence.

'No,' she said, 'I don't think I can explain. I'll have to try
another time. Besides I didn't come to ask whether education
made people happier or unhappier. All I wanted to know was
whether I could be educated without leaving home.'

'You can,' said Pierre. 'You can educate yourself
anywhere and by yourself as long as you have some books
and access to more.'

'But you'd have to know which books and I was counting
on your telling me.'

'It will be very easy to do so once you have told me what it
is you already know and what you don't. Your father was an
educated man and he had some excellent books. He often
told me you were lazy-minded and had no leanings towards
scholarship. Since you were delicate, he did not want to
persuade you, against your will, to give up the outdoor
activities you seemed to love so much more than anything
else.'

'And still do,' replied Marianne. 'As long as I am outdoors and can muse over what I'm doing, I'm all right. If I start thinking hard about it, I nearly die.'

'Come now, my child, then you must stay as you are and continue to live as you do now. I don't see why you should be looking for new occupations when marriage will provide some very serious ones for you.'

'If I marry!' replied Marianne. 'If I don't marry, I'd still like to learn how to spend time when I'm no longer able to run about as I please. But look, it's almost sunset already. Do you want a game of draughts, Madame André?'

Madame André accepted, and Pierre, who hated games of all sorts, stayed in the garden, walking on the terrace and looking at Marianne in the drawing room with his mother. In the soft light of a small green-shaded lamp, she remained as engaged in her game, as naturally unobtrusive and as impassive as ever. Who knows, thought Pierre, whether her intelligence is not held back by a particular kind of nervous condition? Many talented young people never develop to the full for lack of the physical capacity necessary for intellectual work. In women, you take no notice of these organizational failures, so to speak. They follow different courses and achieve different results. Only rarely are women themselves required to make sustained intellectual effort. How is it that Marianne is so determined to be the exception among women? Could it be that, like myself, she is consumed by the inner torment of never having realized her own potential? This is not a female predicament, surely? Woman has another aim in life. For her, being a wife and mother brings its own pride and happiness.

At nine o'clock, Marianne embraced Madame André and shook hands with her godfather. Suzon inclined her legs as trained and Marianne leapt nimbly on to her back. Both horse and rider were so light that the sound of their gallop across the sandy soil was soon lost in the silence of the night. The evening was warm and balmy. Pierre remained for a long time at the gate of his house, following Marianne in his mind's eye. He went with her in his imagination through the little beechwood, the fragrant heathland, past the dark boulders and clear waters of the brook. He thought he could see the world through her eyes and was pleased to endow her with secret feelings possibly not her own.

The following day was a Saturday and market day at the town of La Faille. It is the custom among both peasants and farmers to go to market whether one has anything to buy or sell or not. It is here that people from the outlying districts can meet and do business but it is also the place where news is relayed and the price of commodities established.

Pierre used to go there to read the papers. One visit a week was enough to keep a man retired from active life in touch with events in general. Pierre was passing in front of the Chêne Verte hotel just as the carriage used by travellers from the local diligences was arriving. From the carriage he saw a handsome young man alight and come striding towards him.

'Hello there, here I am!' he cried, falling on Pierre's neck in a fond and familiar embrace. This young Hercules had a complexion as fresh as a rose and was dressed in the latest style of simple and elegant travel wear. It was Philippe Gaucher, who had arrived a day earlier than expected.

'Yes, my dear fellow,' he said, thinking André's bewildered expression meant he was unrecognized, 'it is I, Philippe!'

Pierre interrupted him.

'I can see that perfectly well,' he said, lowering his voice, 'but it's not a good idea to shout your name from the rooftops hereabouts. Your mission will never succeed unless you are discreet. One thing you must learn about the country, my young Parisian friend, is that the best recipe for failure is to let people know your business. Look, we'll go straight on to my house, bypassing the town itself. We'll follow this little lane here. We're nearly in the country already and after an hour's walk, we'll be at my house in time for dinner.'

'An hour's walk with this suitcase?' said Philippe, amazed at the suggestion.

'Is it heavy?' asked Pierre, lifting it. 'Oh, no, no weight at all.'

'But I've got other things as well. There's all my painting equipment. I'm rather hoping to do some work while I'm here.'

'In that case, I'll tell them at the hotel to send all your baggage with a man and a handcart. I myself have no form of transport to offer you. I use shanks's pony and am none the worse for it.'

'Well, of course. Couldn't agree more! Any good landscape painter is always a good walker. I'm quite used to carrying my easel and the rest of my materials on my back too. I'll show you all that tomorrow. For today, the man with a handcart would be very welcome.'

'Wait for me here,' said Pierre.

He proceeded to the hotel to give his orders. Five minutes later he rejoined his guest and they set off together on foot. Philippe's first words greatly astonished Pierre.

'Pretty women in these parts?'

'Look around you,' replied Pierre, laughing.

'That's precisely what I do,' said the painter. 'It's a lifelong habit of mine. And as it happens, I've just seen a rather attractive little person on horseback. Demure as a mouse – the horse, of course.'

'Was she on her own?' asked André, suddenly worried.

'She was indeed. On a little dark grey with a black mane.'

Though it was obvious to whom Philippe was referring, André pretended not to understand.

'Pretty, you said?'

'I couldn't really tell, she went past in a flash. But she looked very charming, yes.'

'She's not generally considered pretty and she herself makes no great claims on that score.'

'You know who I mean?'

'Yes. I think so. Small you say?'

'Small and slim as a rake but very graceful. Dark, curly hair, pale and interesting, you might say; beautiful big eyes.'

'You liked the look of her, then?'

'What I've seen, yes. Why? This isn't . . . is this . . . ? Good heavens!'

'Yes indeed. She is the young lady your father would like you to marry.'

'That's Mademoiselle Chevreuse? Well, well, well! To think I just bumped into her straightaway, like that! Does she know I'm . . . ?'

'She knows nothing whatsoever,' replied Pierre curtly. 'I wasn't even expecting you myself until tomorrow morning.'

'Ah, that's right, of course. I left a day earlier so as to avoid travelling overnight. Painters want to be able to see everything. And on top of that, of course, I wanted to have some general idea of what the countryside's like around here. Here in my native land as it were. I was born at La Faille, you see, just like you, my dear fellow. However, I can remember nothing of my early years here. I must say the town itself, or at least what I've seen of it, looks appalling, but the surrounding countryside is lovely. Before our very eyes, this beautiful green lane, blue horizons in the distance, all quite delightful. I'm sure I'll soon get used to all the misshapen walnut trees round here and those hacked and mutilated elms of yours have a certain comic charm, I have to admit. Yes indeed, by heavens, I mean to be very happy here, I can assure you. And if my wife wants to, we can spend all our summers here.'

'What wife, pray?' said Pierre despite himself and unable to keep irritation out of the disdainful glance he threw the young painter.

'Why, Mademoiselle Chevreuse or someone,' replied Philippe without a moment's hesitation. 'I have come to this place with strict orders from my father to find a wife, and a dowry to boot. If I'm not too particular, that is. I'm tired of being under my father's thumb. He's a good sort, of course, but he can get a bit much sometimes. He and I don't always see eye to eye on certain things. If I double my income by marrying, he'll stop carping and criticizing me for wanting to go in for painting. On with the marriage, say I! Marriage and painting are synonymous, to my father's way of thinking.'

'And because of your great love of painting you will feel bound to your wife, whoever she may turn out to be?'

'No, but I shall be very tolerant. I shan't expect her to be a raving beauty or a marvellous wit. She would have to have a very mean character indeed not to get on with me. I am the best dough kneaded by the Great Baker! I am always cheerful and gay, a lover of light, liberty and laughter. But just a minute! Isn't that the little rider we were just talking about? Look in front! Isn't that Mademoiselle Chevreuse ahead of us? Let's catch up with her quickly so I can have a good look at her!'

XII

Marianne had indeed come to a halt. At least she had slowed Suzon down to a trot so as to be able to talk to the farmer's wife, Marichette, as they travelled together along the Dolmor lane. Marichette was sitting on some sacks of barley in the back of an old ox-cart. Her husband, on foot and carrying a small crop, was leading them at a gentle pace. The lane was too narrow for a horse or even a pedestrian to overtake and squeeze between the wheels and the hedge. Suzon could smell her newly bought barley. Craftily stretching her neck, she nuzzled ingratiatingly in the lap of the farmer's wife. Marichette stroked the horse's forehead and chatted to her mistress about the sheep she had sold to the butcher and the pigs she had haggled over without success.

During the conversation, Marianne had looped the reins loosely over her arm. She sat looking lost in thought and a little tired. Suddenly spotting a beautiful branch of honeysuckle entwined within a bush, she heeled Suzon forward and stretched out her arms to pluck it down. At that moment, young Philippe, having left André behind and crept imperceptibly up on Marianne, leaped up towards the honeysuckle, broke it off easily and with the self-assurance of a born Parisian, presented it to her.

As soon as she saw this handsome stranger with the sparkling eyes and the winning smile, Marianne knew it must be her future suitor. Such gallantry was beyond anyone she knew in the neighbourhood. She blushed a little. Then, immediately recovering, she declined the proffered bouquet with a faint smile, saying:

'Thank you, monsieur; it was not for me but for my horse. She happens to be very fond of honeysuckle.'

'In that case,' replied the painter, equal to the occasion, 'I shall offer it to your horse, who will surely not refuse it!'

He presented the branch to Suzon who promptly and unceremoniously snatched it between her teeth. Philippe had raised his hat high in an exaggerated flourish as Marianne took up the reins again. She made a brief acknowledgement, without looking at Philippe, and urged her horse on. Suzon plunged up to her knees into the ditch, then, swiftly and nimbly skimming past the hubs of the cartwheels and the oxen's horns, she disappeared at a gallop round the corner.

Pierre was grateful to Marianne for this clever exit. The slightest hesitation would have immediately placed Philippe on top of the situation.

'So,' he said with an ironic smile, 'you managed to have a good look at her, did you?'

'Charming!' replied Philippe. 'The very essence of distinction, of wit and self-confidence. Attractive too! A real woman! How old did you say? My father says she's older than I am but he must be joking. She looks like a schoolgirl.'

'She's twenty-five.'

'She can't be!'

'I promise you. She's not at all coy about her age.'

'Well, that's fine by me. You're as old as you look. Take me; bearded monster that I am, you'd never say she was as old as I am. We would make a fine couple of models for a portrait of Strength and Beauty, or some other classical theme like that.'

'So you've made up your mind, have you?'

'Of course! I'm already in love with her!'

'No doubts about your chances?'

'None whatever!'

'It must be good to feel so sure.'

'My dear André, I have two things in my favour, youth and love. They are two very important forces. Love truly felt is always communicated. And youth gives confidence to take risks, to express oneself. I can say without false modesty, I'm young and in love and that's all there is to it.'

'You are right,' said Pierre, suddenly sad and downcast. 'The stupid ones are those who have lost the freshness of youth and whose experience has robbed them of the capacity for simple, instinctive action.'

Close to Pierre's house they had come to a spot where the road widened and they could overtake the cart. Further along the same road, but higher still, they could see Marianne now slowed down again to walking pace.

'She has stopped galloping,' said Philippe. 'Who knows, she might be thinking about me!'

She most certainly is, said Pierre to himself, as his heart began to break.

XIII

Philippe Gaucher found himself under a grave disadvantage:
Madame André loathed the sight of him. He was a good
enough fellow; honest, sincere and with a spirit as open as his
countenance. But Madame André could not allow anyone to
be more handsome than her son, particularly if he did not
possess what passes in the provinces for desirable features:
broad shoulders, black beard, healthy colour or a large chest.
Pierre was interesting, intelligent and modest. His face, like
his entire personality, breathed distinction. This was what
his mother, at least, believed. She had not mixed a great deal
with the world and her ideas concerning what made a man
distinguished or not were somewhat limited in consequence.
However, she was shocked by a certain vulgarity which
pervaded every word, every gesture and every expression of
Philippe's. She came to the conclusion that he was behaving
true to type. She was not lacking in the kind of humour
common to the Berry and its womenfolk in particular. All
through dinner, she kept up a stream of banter which he did
not deign to acknowledge. And in truth, since the obligations
of hospitality overrode all others in her, she had in fact
extended him an extremely warm welcome and anticipated
his every need.

When Philippe learned that the Andrés were to lunch
the following day with Mademoiselle Chevreuse and that
they would take that opportunity of introducing him to
her, he believed that his suit was even more advanced than
he had dared hope. He remarked that his lucky star must

be in the ascendant.

'I wonder which one that might be,' said Madame André, not without malice.

'I don't know the name of it,' said Philippe gaily, 'I am no good at astronomy. But I am looking at the brightest and the most beautiful and I'm sure that one's mine. Do you believe in the stars, Pierre?'

'Well, I suppose so, for people like Napoleon and yourself. If a mere mortal like myself is under some kind of benign astral influence, my star must be so tiny and so remote that I have never been able to spot it.'

Unaware that the old lady was accustomed to retiring at nine o'clock, Philippe had prolonged the evening later than the custom at Dolmor. Seeing the time approach eleven, Pierre said to his guest:

'You must be tired after your long journey. Do tell me when you would like me to show you to your room.'

'I am never tired,' replied Gaucher, 'nothing ever tires me. But I can still feel the pitch and roll of that old coach in my head. It's rocking me to sleep a little, so if you would be so kind . . .'

Pierre led him to a little guest room, newly decorated and very cool. The painter opened the shutters so as to be awakened, he said, as soon as dawn broke. He was anxious to explore the countryside around and to choose a theme for his painting in the days to come.

'Sleep well,' said Pierre. 'I wake at first light and I shall come and call you, if you like, and take you to the most beautiful spots in our valley.'

'Thanks,' replied Philippe, 'but frankly, I prefer to discover these things on my own. An artist likes to make his own judgement in these matters without taking too much into account the opinions of others.'

That means, thought Pierre André, that you are going to satisfy your curiosity by going and pestering Marianne herself. Well, I'll be watching you, my lad! She's not yours yet. As her godfather, I'm still under an obligation to protect her.

He returned to his room and, intending to vent his spleen in writing, he looked, in vain, for the notebook begun the previous day. It was nowhere to be found. Since he could not remember what he had written, he was a little anxious to think he might have lost it during his walk. He remembered that when he returned, he had put down his stick and his bag in the salon. He went downstairs to look and, to his surprise, found his mother there, also a little agitated.

'And what are you looking for, if I may make so bold?' she asked.

'A scruffy little notebook I write things in.'

'It's in here,' she said, opening a drawer. 'I found it this morning and locked it away in there.'

'If you read any of it,' said André, putting the notebook in his pocket, 'you must think me a real idiot.'

'I? Read it? But of course not, gracious heaven! Reading doesn't come easily to me. But why would I think you were an idiot?'

'Because . . . but tell me first, what's made *you* so upset, mother?'

'I can tell you easily enough,' she answered. 'I am furious to think we're going to have to introduce this young fool to Marianne and that, since we've put him up and given him a welcome, we will have to pretend in front of her that he's absolutely charming, that's why I'm angry! Well I won't do it! I cannot be so hypocritical. I find him an insufferable little whippersnapper. I can't promise not to show what I think of him to her, I warn you.'

'Perhaps you're judging him too hastily,' replied Pierre, sitting next to his mother, who had thrown herself irritably onto the couch. 'He's not a fool and he's not nasty. The way he behaves – his manner – though we may think it over-confident, may well be pleasing to Marianne. Who can say? Marianne may not be as particular as you think. She may not have all the good sense that you and I through you attributed to her.'

'Marianne has plenty of spirit,' protested Madame André, 'and a lot of good sense. You don't know her.'

'That's true. She's a mystery to me.'

'Your fault. You hardly ever speak to her. And you're so bad at making the most of opportunities to get to know her.'

'It is partly my fault, but a lot more hers. I tell you she loves playing the sphinx. I haven't the gall of a Philippe Gaucher, to lift the veil of modesty that protects a young girl. For all she is a child to me, she is still a woman and I hope I shall never invade any woman's reserve.'

XIV

Madame André thought for a few minutes then took her son's hand and said:

'You are too timid! Far too timid! If you had wanted it, it's you that Marianne would have loved! You and you alone she would have married.'

'That's an old story. That was six years ago. Just think. Six years ago I had to give up any idea of marrying.'

'Why? Was thirty-five too old to get married?'

'Old enough to judge one's future in the light of past experience. If you haven't made your mark by the age of thirty-five, you may as well admit you never will. Get out of people's way. Forget all the trials and tribulations.'

'All the more reason to get married.'

'I don't think of love as a means to a good marriage. Nor will I ever.'

'Yes, yes, I understand. I know you. I have some pride too. I can understand yours. What I do hold against you, though, is the fact that you have never loved Marianne for herself. She deserved it and she was well-disposed towards you.'

'That's true but I didn't think it possible Marianne could love me. If Philippe Gaucher has too much self-confidence, my fault is in having too little, perhaps. And of course I must admit I was very interested in travelling again. Someone other than myself, with a bit more wit and *savoir-faire* would have been able to make the most of the opportunities given me. But I've told you a hundred times, I'm my own worst enemy. Now that everything's over, I'm glad to be able at least to give you a little happiness. Let's not spoil the present with all these hopeless, futile recriminations. You say Marianne might have loved me. She must know that I have not been aware of this, and she'll never forgive me. Now I understand why she is so cold towards me, the formal language, everything. However sweet and calm a woman is on the surface, she never easily forgives a man for having been blind. Now that she is drawn into the adoring gaze of this purposeful young man, she would be wise to avenge herself for my stupidity. Ah, sweet revenge! Long may she be happy! We can wish for no more. I shall try to behave philosophically and approve of her choice without reservation.'

'How wrong you are, Pierre! There's still time if only you want her. You can't want her! You can't love my poor Marianne! Oh what a loss for her. You could have made her so happy. Happier than she could ever be with such a creature. She's worth ten of him any day!'

'If she *is* as superior as you like to think, she will no doubt understand before it's too late. She still hasn't said yes.'

'You still doubt her intelligence! Oh you stupid man! Forgive me. I know you are bound to think I have no judgement in these matters. But I do know how impossible it is to guess what someone's nature is like if all they do is hide it all the time. But when you *want* to love someone, you look. When you love, you see. If you really loved . . .'

Pierre kissed his mother's hand with fervour and instantly regretted it. He had nearly told her that, for the past few days, he had been hopelessly in love. If he confessed how he was feeling, she would suffer too and would push him into a fight he dared not believe he could win.

'We'll talk about this again tomorrow,' he said to her.

'Let's just see how old Gaucher gets on. It's late. We must get some sleep. Don't worry. Just know that I am happy enough living with you. I don't really want a great deal more.'

Once back in his room, Pierre decided to try and express all this emotion in writing and opened his notebook once more. On the page where he had written the previous day, he found a little wild pansy he could not remember having placed there. It set him dreaming.

It should be possible to make a little herbarium of experiences he said to himself. A flower, a sprig of this, some moss, could become as precious as relics if they reminded one of the great events of the inner life, moments of great emotion or great perception. People remember the risks and dangers of picking certain specimens. Huge vistas of the world unfold before us as before: yet they only reflect time in the external world. How different would be the vision of the soul's unfolding.

At that moment, Pierre heard footsteps on the echoing wood of the corridors and stairs of his cottage, then the sound of a door being opened downstairs. Through the window he saw Philippe Gaucher apparently setting off in the middle of the night to find a suitable theme for his painting.

XV

It was one o'clock in the morning. The conversation between Pierre and his mother summarized very briefly above had continued for more than two hours. On what whim, Pierre asked himself, was the young artist stepping out of the house and now the paddock before the light of day? In order to assure his own independence as quickly and as effectively as possible, this young fool was using all means at his disposal to compromise Marianne. Anger surged into André's breast. In a few moments, he had joined the young man, who was now walking with a resolute step in the direction of Validat.

'And where do you think you're going?' he asked brusquely. 'Are you sleepwalking by any chance?'

'Ah, yes,' replied Philippe, more surprised than angered by his host's solicitude. 'The sleepwalk of love! Heading directly and instinctively towards its object. I shall be able to find my own way to the lovely maiden's abode, thank you. This is where I saw her disappear yesterday. You told me she lived not far off the road near the hills on the right. It's a clear night and in an hour it will be dawn. Don't worry about me, my dear chap. I should hate to put you out in any way.'

'I should indeed be put out if the welfare of any of my dearest friends were in jeopardy as is now the case.'

'But you're really too kind! I would honestly prefer to go alone, I do assure you . . .'

'I beg your pardon but as it happens I was thinking more of my god-daughter than of yourself.'

'Your god-daughter? Who's that?'

'Why, Mademoiselle Chevreuse, of course. And it is she, if I am not much mistaken, that you seem to want to compromise by this behaviour.'

'Your god-daughter, is she? Well, well, well! Now all is clear. I took you for a jealous rejected suitor. Now that I know you to be some kind of father to her, I must, of course, acknowledge your right to protect her. I do assure you I should be more sorry than I can say to compromise your Marianne. Do be sure, my dear friend, that I have nothing but the most honourable of intentions. Let me tell you what I planned. Yesteday our young lady refused to accept some flowers from me. She claimed she only wanted them for her horse – that's the mare, Suzon, you told me about last night. So this morning, what I'm going to do is ransack all the hedges around here for honeysuckle, make a wonderful garland of it to entwine around Mademoiselle Chevreuse's door and write a note to go with it saying: "To Mademoiselle Suzon from her devoted servant". So you see, there's nothing to worry about. Your god-daughter will just laugh at the whole thing.'

'If you really want her to laugh, go ahead with that idea.'

'You mean you're hoping she'll laugh at me. Makes no difference! The main thing is to keep her thinking about me. Laughing with or at, it doesn't matter. Make me ridiculous! I'll be grateful to you! When her head is completely turned by all these mad gestures of love I shall reap the benefit. I plan to do all sorts of wild things but always such that her dutiful godfather will never have to remind me of the respect I owe his ward.'

Pierre was inclined to tell him immediately that the gift for Suzon was the equivalent of a declaration of love to Marianne and moreover, one which would give rise to as much gossip as if he had deposited a traditional crown of may, the local token of engagement. But Philippe seemed so determined that Pierre could either let him go or show him his own anger. The latter course was both unwise and inhospitable. He therefore pretended to take the scheme lightheartedly and allowed him to go on alone. Before doing so, he reminded him that Madame André would have breakfast ready at nine, that they would leave at about midday for the meal at Validat which would take place, according to local custom, at about three in the afternoon.

'Don't worry about me,' replied Philippe. 'I beg of you not to wait for me. If I am too far away to return by breakfast time I can always beg a crust of bread and some milk from somewhere. The landscape artist is never at a loss! I have made enough excursions outside your tiny perfect little county to know this much.'

Pierre made as if to return but, instead, cut across the fields to Validat itself. He wanted to observe the progress of the man he now called privately and not without disdain his protégé.

He burst into happy laughter a quarter of an hour later, as he saw Philippe stop at the junction of the low road leading to Validat and continue on the high road towards the manor of Mortsang. Philippe had looked down at the moss-covered rooftiles of the Validat farm, nestling modestly under the walnut trees with never a turret or a balcony in sight. He had clearly thought it impossible that the lady of his dreams could live in such unprepossessing surroundings. Spotting an imposing manor house, it was to the new gentry within that he was now preparing to make his gift of love.

XVI

Determined nevertheless to keep good watch over Marianne, Pierre returned to the house to pick up his stick and his bag. These were the necessary accoutrements of his daily excursions, without which people would have been surprised to see him wander the countryside. In that part of the world it is frowned upon to ramble without a proper objective; you would be thought mad. But if you appear to be looking for something or to be collecting something, you pass for a scholar, which is not quite as bad, unless, of course, a suspicious aura of black magic surrounds you! Pierre was sufficiently knowledgeable about country ways to look as if he knew what he was about. Besides, since he was interested in ruins, and plants and rocks, he was understood to be working for the government in some way or other on regional statistics. It would never occur to a peasant or a farmer in the middle of France that an individual might undertake research for his or her own pleasure or edification.

The sun had risen when Pierre André found himself in the beech grove of the ravine beneath Validat. There, hidden in a copse, he could keep an eye on the farmhouse and on the lanes leading to it. He noticed much bustle around the farmhouse itself, probably preparations for the luncheon later on in the day. At about five o'clock, he saw Marianne herself out in the yard giving instructions and going in and out of the house. Presently, Suzon was brought to her. She mounted, and rode off through the wood towards the brook. Pierre ran down the hill and reached the little ford just as she did.

'And where are you off to so early in the morning?' he said in a peremptory tone that took her by surprise.

'If you really want to know, I'm going up to Mortsang to get some butter. I like to think that you shall want for nothing at the table today. . . !'

'Send someone else, Marianne, I beg of you. Don't go to Mortsang, don't go anywhere today! Stay at home and wait for us to come. Tomorrow you can decide whether or not to continue riding about alone.'

'I don't understand.'

'You mean you do not wish to understand. Let me tell you. Philippe Gaucher left Dolmor in the middle of the night to bring you a bunch of flowers. He mistook the house and went on with it to Mortsang or somewhere else in that direction. If you go there this morning you run the risk of meeting him.'

'And what if I did?'

'That is your affair. I will have warned you, that is all. If you want to be seen running after him . . .'

'Why should anyone think I was anxious to see him?'

'Never mind, that is what he himself will think.'

'You surely don't think he's so stupid.'

'I did not say so. It is for you to decide but he has a good deal of self-confidence. That you must have noticed already.'

'Self-confidence, yes. There's a difference between being self-confident and being ridiculous. Tell me about him, please. I will leave today's errands to someone else since you prefer. I'll go back and say Suzon has begun to limp and I didn't want to make her go on, but please let's talk a little. It's so lucky that we met like this.'

'Not luck at all, I have been watching you.'

'Really? Watching *me*?'

'Yes, you. I have to give you advice and protection until

such time as you will come to me and say, "I know this young man and he is the one for me." That time may well come tonight or tomorrow morning. At the rate Philippe goes about things I dare say my guardianship will not be needed for much longer.'

'You think I will come to know him by tonight or tomorrow? I fear you credit me with far too much intelligence.'

'My dear, I do wish you would stop playing silly games.'

'Oh,' cried Marianne, listening and paying closer attention than usual to Pierre. 'Please continue; explain me to myself, that's all I ask. Are you saying I'm pretending to be silly and I am really not?'

Pierre was embarrassed by such a direct and unexpected question.

'I did not come here to dissect you,' he replied. 'My role as your godfather requires me simply to maintain your respectability in the eyes of others. But you wish me to speak about Monsieur Philippe. You who are so indifferent to all other topics show great curiosity on his account! Well, then, all I have to say about him is that he is enterprising and that he is determined to use every means at his disposal to find favour in your eyes.'

'Favour in my eyes? You mean he likes me?'

'So he says.'

'But he doesn't mean it?'

'I do not know. I should not like to think he sought you other than for your own sake.'

'What has he said about me? He does not know me. He cannot find me attractive.'

'On the contrary, he does.'

'But he doesn't mean it, does he? Tell me, I beg of you.'

As she plied him with these questions, Marianne's face had come to life. She looked in turn both resolute and frightened. She blushed and from time to time her eyes flashed. It was a real transformation and Pierre was greatly struck by it.

'You love him already,' he replied. 'Look at you, you've become pretty. He has brought a beauty into you that was not there before.'

'If he brings me beauty,' said Marianne, flushing deeply with pleasure, 'it's a lovely gift and I'm very grateful to him for it. I've always thought myself plain and no one has disabused me of the notion.'

'You have never been plain and I do not believe I ever . . .'

'Oh *you*,' she answerd, quickly. 'You've never looked at me. You wouldn't know what I'm like.'

'Coquette again, Marianne, you see? I have always considered you with . . . interest.'

'Yes, like a doctor looking at a patient. You thought I wouldn't live and now that you see me blooming with health you need no longer trouble yourself on my account.'

'And yet, you know, I did not sleep last night, for worrying about you.'

'Worrying? Why should you worry? What possible dangers could Monsieur Philippe Gaucher be to me? He's an honest man, isn't he? Young enough not to be insincere. And besides, I'm not so much of a child as to be taken in by pretty speeches by any young man.'

'No, there's only the danger that people might talk, before you decided to let it be known . . . You of all people, so mindful of public opinion that you will now allow me to come and visit you in your home . . .'

'But that would be much more serious. Everyone knows you would never marry me. You're not in the same position as a young man beginning to set himself up in the world.'

'What nonsense are you talking? Would I not marry you, if

ever I were so unfortunate as to compromise you?'

'Of course you would. You would do precisely that and marry me out of honour. But I should not like either to place you in such embarrassment or to be forced to accept marriage as some form of alternative.'

Everything that Marianne said troubled Pierre deeply. They had stopped, she in midstream, astride Suzon who was drinking and he leaning against some sandstone rock. The river flowing clear between them seemed hardly to touch its sandy bed. Trees, standing close together and covered with new young leaves, cast over all a greenwood shade in which was mingled the rose of the rising sun.

'Marianne,' said André, now pensive, 'you are extremely beautiful this morning. The young squire who was clever enough to discover your beauty first will have the greatest contempt for me. I spoke of you to him modestly, like a father receiving compliments on his daughter. He will be bound to tell you . . .'

'And what should I think?'

'You should remember that a man in my position could not look at you as an aspiring lover might and that he is not to be scoffed at for keeping faith with himself. You seem to be criticizing me for having been blind through disdain or through indifference. Could you not see I have been so out of honesty of heart and out of respect for you?'

'Thank you,' replied Marianne with a radiant smile. 'You have never hurt me by your indifference. I care little whether I am thought beautiful provided I am loved and I am sure enough of your loyal friendship for that. If Monsieur Gaucher is not a suitable match for me you have only to tell me so and I shall do only what you think best.'

'Let us wait till this evening, Marianne. If you like him, everything will be different and you will no longer want my advice.'

'I could like him and you not . . . So much the worse – even then I would still listen to you.'

'You must not joke, my child. If he suits you, I will have to approve of him.'

Marianne's expression changed and she suddenly became once more the cold little person Pierre knew of old. Her godfather's resignation had wounded her and, despairing of ever kindling a spark of love in his heart, she seemed finally to be abandoning once and for all the hope of being loved by him.

'Since you grant me such freedom of conscience,' she said, 'from now on I shall take care to keep only my own counsel. Until tonight, then.'

She was about to retrace her steps when Pierre, overcome by sudden emotion, seized hold of the bridle and cried:

'Wait, Marianne! You cannot leave the echo of those icy words in my ears!'

'What then?' said Marianne, softening. 'What would you like me to say?'

'A word of affection. A word of trust.'

'Didn't you hear me promise not to marry against your wishes?'

'And will you not understand that I cannot accept the sacrifice of your submission?'

'Perhaps it would not be a sacrifice, who knows?'

'Who knows, indeed? And least of all yourself, as yet.'

And just at the moment when he might have given way to the flood of feeling rising within him, Pierre, abashed and forlorn, let fall the horse's bridle. He lowered his face but too late to hide from Marianne the sight of his eyes brimming with tears.

XVII

At last, thought Marianne to herself as she began the walk back to her home, now I think I see how things stand. I really thought he would never love me. For did he not think and write that marriage was a tomb and that he could never be satisfied merely with the peaceful contentment it brings? And yet he is sad when he sees me hesitate. What a peculiar character he is. What a Doubting Thomas!

She entered the house and shut herself up in her room, prey to the strangest emotions she had ever experienced. Honest with herself as always, she recognized that meeting Philippe had affected her deeply. Her instinct had been to bask in the admiration of this stranger. People with decided views spare the rest of us a good deal of trouble, she thought. They are very frank about themselves and save everyone else from having to break down any barriers of reserve. The fact is, Pierre respects me. That's all very flattering but doesn't he carry it a little too far? Does he really want me to make all the advances? Isn't it in the natural order of things that he take the initiative?

Marianne felt herself falling into the ancient trap, the old inclination of her sex to prize the masculine resolve of the other. She had thrilled with pleasure when Pierre had masterfully seized the bridle of her horse to prevent her from escaping. Philippe, however, would never have let it go. Pierre's courage had lasted only a moment. Yet the tears he had been unable to control would never have been shed by Philippe.

Perhaps it is my timidity and not his that is to blame, she said to herself. I have never been able to say a word, never let him guess by so much as a glance that I want his love. I am too proud and he thinks me stupid or indifferent. Perhaps he would really love me if I could be a little bolder, who knows?

Meanwhile, since there was no more need to watch over Philippe's movements, Pierre made his way back to Dolmor. Tears poured slowly, unnoticed, down his cheeks. So this is to be my fate always, he said to himself. My folly of follies is to be in love with the impossible. As long as Marianne was free and seemed indifferent, I never gave her a moment's thought. The minute a worthy rival appears, who seems to put me out of the running, I become desperately jealous. My stupidity verges on the lunatic. At the very time I should speak out I feel more than ever the impossibility of doing so!

He found his mother already up and making breakfast. Rather than not speak of Marianne at all, he began to tell his mother about his meeting with her earlier in the day. He added:

'Marianne is a flirt, you know. She's making cruel sport of me, I can tell you! She wants me to say I am in love with her. She needs this as her revenge; then, tonight or tomorrow night, she'll be able to have a good laugh at my expense with her husband-to-be.'

Madame André's efforts to convince him this was not true fell on deaf ears. She went so far as to maintain that his little neighbour had loved no one else but him, that it was for him alone that she was waiting as she had for the previous five or six years. But she could not, in all honesty, say she had heard this from Marianne's own lips and Pierre rejected all hope as the most dangerous trap of all. He would not admit that his heart was ensnared and in the end his mother cried impatiently:

'Let's resign ourselves to it, then! If this marriage of hers makes us sad, if we hate the prospect of it, we will just have to tell ourselves we did nothing to stop it!'

Philippe arrived for breakfast and did it honour. He told Pierre how he had taken a wrong turning before finding Validat and that he had very nearly hung the garland of honeysuckle on the gates of Mortsang by mistake. He had found out just in time the name of the place and the people who lived there. Then he had walked further and got lost in some swampy marshland before finding his way again. At about eight o'clock in the morning, he had come to a modest-looking farmhouse. He was on the point of passing by when he saw a little horse grazing in a field nearby and recognized her. He had managed to get into the field through a hedge of thorns, placed the garland on the mare's scrawny little neck and returned in triumph. His efforts had been crowned with success and the night, in his opinion, well spent.

Pierre scarcely replied. In order to get rid of him, he suggested Philippe might like to lie down. He might want to restore his energy lest lack of sleep spoil his chances of success in the struggle to come. Philippe swore he could go without sleep for three nights in a row without ill-effect. This did not prevent his discreetly stretching out in the mossy hollow of a tree and savouring the delights of slumber till nearly noon.

At the stroke of twelve, the cart and the mare from the Validat farm arrived at the gate of Dolmor. Madame André had dressed in her purple silk which, though ten years old, was still like new. Philippe put on a beautifully cut black suit and a dazzling white cravat. Pierre put on his normal Sunday best. Madame André climbed into the cart which Marichette's husband led at walking pace by the mare's side. Philippe, sitting by Madame André, made the motions of driving. Despite all his best efforts, he never did succeed in leading the quiet country-bred horse into the fashionable trot he desired.

Pierre went ahead on foot. Arriving first at Validat he waited for the cart to arrive before going in. The heavy old vehicle lumbered slowly and majestically through the already opened gate and came to a halt between the farmhouse door and the dunghill. Philippe found his future manor a little too rustic and vowed to change all this, however little scope there was for improvement. Unfortunately, there was in fact none, and Marianne, waiting for her guests at the threshold of the farmhouse itself, received them all with neither more nor less ceremony than she would a simple peasant. Although she had a charming room of her own on the other side of the dividing wall, she was not disposed to admit strangers to it yet and Pierre was grateful to her for not allowing their new guest in quite so soon.

Having kissed Madame André, shaken hands with her godfather and greeted the newcomer with confidence, Marianne led the first into her room so as to relieve her of her shawl and her black veil. These were the days when the shabby-genteel of the country rarely wore hats and put a veil instead over their white linen bonnets.

XVIII

Pierre was secretly amused by Philippe's discomfiture which
he hid as best he could under a kind of banter. He himself
loved the simplicity, not to say the primitiveness, of local
country custom and Marianne had obviously changed
nothing of the old ways of her childhood.

For a long time she had had no other living room than this,
with its smoke-blackened beams from which hung bunches
of golden onions and in the middle, lantern-like, a swinging
wicker cage for holding cheeses. The cleanliness of peasants
hereabouts is legendary and, although chickens and ducks
wander in at all times, they and their traces are constantly
chased away by the housewife armed with a broom. The beds
and all the furniture are polished and shining and dishes
gleam on the dresser. But these cane beds, with their covers
of yellow serge faded to the colour of dead leaves, the black
fireplace with its clutter of hanging pots and pans, the cats
and the children everywhere, the cracked, uneven floor, the
single small window, and the ceiling crowded with dangling
utensils and provisions, were very far from the young
Parisian's dream of domestic bliss. Even in his imagination,
he could not transform these low and dimly lit surroundings
into an artist's workshop. Shrewdly keeping up the jovial
tone with which he had begun, he let slip not one word that
might reveal to Pierre the full extent of his disappointment.
He confined himself to asking whether this was where they
would be dining.

'I presume so,' replied Pierre. 'I know that Mademoiselle

Chevreuse has had apartments made for herself somewhere in the house but since their installation I have not been within and I do not know if there is a dining room. I believe she lives on completely equal terms with the farm-workers and that she takes her meals with them.'

'Are we then to eat with all of them? How charming! This is what I call real country living!'

At that moment, Marichette came to tell Pierre that if the gentlemen wished to come into the garden, they would find places to sit and that the young lady was no doubt already there, with Madame André.

'The garden is behind the house,' she added, 'but if you would like to pass through the young lady's apartments, you will be saved the trouble of walking round the house.'

'We prefer to walk round,' replied Pierre, who, though curious to see inside Marianne's rooms, did not wish to set a precedent for his companion. They passed behind the farm buildings and walked into Marianne's garden where they found a table set up on a little patch of sheltered ground next to the house. French windows to the latter were wide open and from the outside they could see a small drawing room with old wood panelling, newly and brilliantly restored, with Louis XV furniture to match.

Making a slight effort, Pierre could recall having seen these same rooms and this same furniture during old Chevreuse's time, but dirty and chipped in those days, neglected and uncared for. Marianne had had the good sense to appreciate these reminders of an earlier age and to have had them restored as new. The floor was covered in a carpet of soft colours, there were no objects on the polished wood shelves but splendid arrangements of flowers gave greenery everywhere, filled all the corners and the space on the console table opposite the fireplace.

'But this is exquisite!' cried Philippe. 'I knew she was an artist.'

'And how, pray!' said Pierre, even more surprised than he.

'My dear fellow, it's the sort of thing you can pick out in a woman from the very first glance. Marianne is an absolute duchess.'

'And what might that mean?' asked Pierre. 'I fear that my acquaintance with the world, unlike your own, is very slight.'

'Is that why you're in such a filthy mood today?' replied Philippe, laughing.

XIX

The arrival of Marianne and Madame André put an end to this conversation. They were coming through the garden and the men went quickly to join them. Pierre announced to his god-daughter that having been banned for so long from her private garden he would no longer recognize it and wished to see the changes she had made.

'But I have made none,' she replied. 'My father loved the garden. He planted it himself and I wanted to destroy none of it. Besides, the farm-workers have to have their rightful share of the produce. With the passage of time, some of the trees have died and the frost has carried off a good many of the old bushes. Local species have grown to take their place and the bottom of the close at the end of the orchard, where my father wanted to make a nursery, has become completely wild.'

'I would love to see it,' said Pierre. 'I remember that it was very wet there and I told your father those ornamental trees would not do well.'

'Do go, but without us,' replied Marianne. 'It's a little too damp and rough for Madame André.'

Pierre crossed the orchard and walked into the old nursery which extended over a strip of land enclosed by very tall hedges and with a small brook flowing through. He was suddenly enraptured. Marianne had allowed nature complete sway over this small natural park, and grass had grown there, tall and dense in places, short and patchy in others, following the course of a number of rivulets which, branching away from the main stream, flowed back in slow meanders through the earth. The soil itself, light and with a rich mixture of fine sand, was particularly good for local flora and every kind of wild plant grew there in great profusion. The water was bright with iris and both white and yellow water-lilies; sturdy clumps of elder and hawthorn stood in abundance around. The ground was a riot of local wild orchids in all their infinite variety and with thousands of other sweet blooms: forget-me-nots of different kinds, campion, grass-of-Parnassus, wild hyacinth, some white and all intoxicating in their fragrance. Where the ground rose and was drier, heather and broom still grew, and here and there within them, the stars, white above and pink below, of wood anemones.

There was no path and only where the loose and sandy soil had fallen in was there room to walk in this confusion of vegetation where no animals strayed, and which was frequented by Marianne alone. There were boulders where she could sit and reflect and clumps of elder and beech provided shade, though not so much as to stifle the growth of small plants at their feet.

She loves nature then, thought Pierre, seized with an inner joy. She understands it, she feels it as I do! She has not said so, nor does she speak of it. But I was sure!

'Well, godfather,' she said, suddenly appearing at his side, 'you see what a dreadful gardener I am. You would never change your new garden, even though it is a little immature, for this old wilderness of a marshland, would you?'

'This old marshland is a paradise to me! Do you know, a botanist could make an almost complete collection of all local flora? I am more than surprised. I have found here the rarest of species, which I have been obliged on occasion to go and look for much farther afield! Here – this, for example, this *elodia* at our feet . . .'

'Oh, that one's from Crevant. Rocky soil. It's been good enough to grow for me here, though.'

'You mean you sometimes go as far as Crevant?'

'Often. It's a very rich natural garden. That's where I found this pretty white hyacinth.'

'It's not a hyacinth, it's a *menyanthes*. Much more beautiful and much rarer.'

'I don't know the names of the plants, but I do know what they look like and I know their fragrance. Every time I go out, I collect seeds and bulbs and I take cuttings. I bring them back here and they nearly all do well.'

'Now I understand! Can I believe that this little Eden is your own creation?'

'Partly mine, but I haven't deliberately propagated all the weeds! People would think me really mad.'

'You might have told me. I am just as mad.'

'Ah, but you're a scholar. It's right and proper for you to collect examples of everything. I know nothing about it so I've no excuse.'

'But why should you need an excuse for loving flowers? Oh Marianne, it's all the more delightful that you should not know all the secrets of their beauty. If you examined them carefully . . .'

'I *do*. I do examine them and although I don't know a thing about botany I can tell you all their characteristics, all their similarities and all their differences. They're so beautiful and so varied. Of course I have greater admiration for the splendid exotica you have in your garden but they are not my friends, as these little wild familiar things are that are so close to me.'

'Do you go looking for them when you are out and about? I imagined you saw nothing, racing away on that horse of yours for the pleasure of going fast. I thought you only loved the country for the sake of speeding through its open spaces.'

'I do love speed, to fly through the wind, like a hare racing over the heath, but what I really prefer is to go at walking pace and stop and look at whatever I like or whatever arouses my curiosity. I like both, the things I know and the things I don't know. I'd like to know everything and learn nothing, or rather . . . I'd like to know everything and then be able to forget it, so I could rediscover it again when I wanted. There is such joy in discovery that if I always knew things, I should be deprived of it.'

'Stay as you are, Marianne! I see you are one of those who possess the truth without having it demonstrated to them. Tell me, since you are so frank about yourself today . . .'

'We must stop. I'm afraid your mother will be getting anxious without me. I left her so as to come and join you here. Let's go back to her now.'

XX

'Will you give me your arm?' said Pierre, tearing himself with regret away from this oasis of flowers where Marianne had for the first time revealed the secret of her solitary thoughts.

'We can't walk two abreast here,' replied Marianne, 'there's room for one person only.'

'One person only . . . that will not be for long. I think you will soon be making this into a path . . .'

'Please let's hurry,' said Marianne. 'Here comes Monsieur Gaucher looking for us. I don't want him to come into my wilderness.' And she began to run, light and nimble over the rough ground she skimmed like a swallow.

'Thank you, Marianne,' Pierre cried in his heart.

But the joy that intoxicated him quickly dissipated when he saw Marianne accept the arm Philippe was offering her, to rejoin Madame André. He wished she could have found a pretext for refusing it, but without affectation, there was no way she could have done so. And she seemed little disposed to play the prude in front of Gaucher. She had dressed rather gaily in a wool-muslin dress of buttercup yellow which showed off her tanned complexion to advantage. Its brightness was softened here and there at the neck and along the arms by ruches of fine and near-transparent tulle. In the thick, short curls of her dark hair, which was more carefully groomed than usual, lay a single yellow rose, tinged with pink. She had on pretty shoes and her feet, normally hidden in ankleboots or heavy walnut-wood sabots, were extraordinarily dainty. Gaucher appraised them with an undisguised boldness she appeared not to find displeasing. He looked at her feet, her hands and her waist, like a connoisseur who wants to make his satisfaction obvious. He did not hesitate to tell her that her dress was ravishing and that her waist was like a palm-tree swaying in the breeze.

'A palm tree? My waist?' replied Marianne, gaily. 'Then it must be a dwarf palm, a *chamaerops*, isn't that so?'

'Oh! Oh! We're a scholar, are we?' cried Philippe.

'Not at all. Monsieur Pierre has a palm like it in his collection. I remember the name.'

'But you do love flowers! These vases and urns you have filled . . . they're marvels of taste!'

'They're only from the fields and hedges, you know. I like them better outdoors than in my little drawing room. But then again, I don't often have the pleasure of receiving Madame André. As the ancients offered sacrifices to their protectors the gods, I sacrifice beautiful flowers to my good friend here.'

'I don't see so much as a sprig of honeysuckle,' said Pierre, who had followed Marianne into the drawing room where Madame André was resting.

'Suzon might have been kind enough to offer me some of hers but since that garland irritated her, she rolled over on top of it. You can well imagine what sort of a state it was in when she'd finished with it. All that remained was the greeting, which of course she had to ignore, little illiterate that she is!'

'You're laughing I see, Monsieur André,' said Philippe to Pierre. 'And why, pray? Don't you see I've achieved my objective?'

'Your objective?' said Marianne.

'Yes, my purpose! I wanted you to know that I had been

thinking of you since long before daybreak. Now you know it. That's all I wanted.'

'And what was it that made you think of me so early in the morning?'

'Do you want me to tell you?'

'Well, since it appears you want me to ask you, yes.'

'May I speak to you like this in public?'

'You have not told me in private that I was the object of your thoughts. One should never begin a public speech that has to be finished in private. Better to say nothing at all.'

'In other words, I should have held my tongue.'

'I'm not saying that. I do want to know what it was that made you think about me this morning. It was no doubt something agreeable, since you started to pay court to Suzon . . .'

'What I thought was that you were gracious and charming enough to turn any fellow's head.'

'Thank you, kind sir! You pay compliments with sovereign assurance. Should I curtsey, do you think?'

'If you wish, Mademoiselle Marianne.'

'There, Monsieur Philippe,' she cried laughingly, and swept into a majestic curtsey of mock-ceremony.

Pierre looked at her, amazed. He had never dreamed she could be so lively and flirtatious. Emboldened, Philippe began to pay court in earnest. He seemed delighted to be the object of her raillery. He thought, as anyone else might have done in his place, that she was taking great pleasure in making him fall in love with her.

XXI

Dinner was served under the vines and the jasmine, whose long fronds, descending over the awning, formed a fringe of flowers round the guests. The table was a colourful display of old pottery valueless at the time and much admired today; their cheerful colours on a blue background were a feast for the eyes. Marianne had set out ancient Nevers glassware that her parents had hidden away as old junk but which a connoisseur would have recognized. Philippe was enough of an artist to appreciate at least the originality of these pretty dishes and he let no occasion slip to praise both the general effect and the details of the service. He ate voraciously. Marichette, under her mistress's guidance, was a superb cook and in her hands the simplest dishes turned into gastronomic delights. In old Chevreuse's cellar there still remained some excellent wines and Marianne had made a superb choice from among them. She had been at pains for the dinner to be as attractive as her own appearance and demeanour.

Philippe, who believed the entire celebration to be in his honour, quickly thought that all augured exceptionally well for his suit and that he would have little trouble in capturing both the heart and the dowry of the young lady. By dessert, though not exactly drunk, he was a little maudlin. Pierre's attempts to restrain him through argument and debate had only served to excite him the more. Madame André, hoping to make a fool of him, had resorted to simple teasing. Marianne had allowed him to be both confiding and expansive.

Her enthusiasm could easily have been taken for encouragement. Indeed, as they rose from the table, after a long stream of gallantries, some well-turned, some decidedly not, Philippe grabbed Marianne's arm and said he would like to see her sheep in the meadow, her cows in the corn. A landscape painter like himself was so much better a judge of these things than a peasant could be, he claimed.

'I don't believe a word of it,' said Marianne, drawing her arm away. 'You seem to think you know more about everything than we do, town and country life alike. And all because you're a painter! I'd venture to suggest that your profession spoils your vision.'

And as Philippe was about to protest, she added:

'You see too much to see properly and you want to translate the untranslatable. Beauty is like God, which exists by itself and gains nothing from all the hymns and paeans of praise lavished upon it. On the contrary, words, hymns, paintings and everything invented to embellish the truth only serve to diminish the feeling one has when one contemplates it without worrying about means of expression.'

'What's all this?' cried Philippe. 'Are you against Art? Are you an out-and-out philistine? Coming from you, these words are like a caterpillar on a rose.'

'Ah, there I have you!' replied Marianne with feeling, 'what is wrong with a caterpillar on a rose, pray? The ones that live on our roses are beautifully fine and smooth, they're a wonderful spring-like green; you have obviously never looked at a caterpillar, Mr Landscape Artist. Some of them are marvellous! I can't think of a single one that's ugly. How can you want to go and look at sheep in the meadow and cows in the corn when you can't even look at a much smaller creature properly?'

'Are you, as a naturalist,' Philippe asked Pierre, 'responsible for persuading your god-daughter that art kills all feeling for nature? If so, you have boxed her into a real paradox, I must say!'

'It's your way of presenting it that makes it seem like a paradox,' replied André, 'and your own argument is no less of a paradox. I think that if we phrased the question better, we could discuss it more fruitfully.'

'Yes, do rephrase it then,' said Marianne.

'Well, this is how it seems to me,' continued Pierre, addressing Gaucher. 'You think that in order to see, one must know what one is looking at. I agree; the naturalist sees better than the peasant. But art is different from science. It has to be felt before it can be expressed. That is what Marianne means. She thinks you have not yet loved nature enough to represent it faithfully. Do remember that neither she nor I have seen any of your paintings, so that it's not your talent that she is criticizing, but your theory, which does seem a little high-handed in a person of your tender age. She thinks you should not start in the studio and then proceed into the country but begin in the countryside before going into the studio. In other words, one doesn't learn how to look at things as a result of being a painter; one learns to become a painter through knowing how to look at things. Isn't that what you wanted to say, Marianne?'

'Absolutely,' she replied. 'So you think I'm right, then?'

'Oh, *do* let's go and look at the animals,' cried Philippe. 'This is altogether too intellectual for me!'

'Very well, let's go and see the animals,' replied Marianne, and, to her godfather, 'Are you coming?'

Then she added in a low voice:

'I'll come with you as far as the byre, then I'm coming back here to keep your mother company.'

'We'll follow you,' replied Pierre.

But follow them he did not. He returned to the salon with Madame André, saying: 'Let them get on with it together. The time has come for Marianne to decide. She wants to. She has given him every encouragement. All he needs to do is roll all the declarations he's been making to her over dinner into one and, if Marianne likes it, what you and I think is neither here nor there. We will simply have to put up with it.'

Madame André was distressed. She did not want Pierre to abandon his suit. She forced him to return to Marianne's side. He promised to obey and went off by himself to the end of the little wilderness where, only a few short hours before, he had felt a moment of hope and happiness. Already that moment was gone. His entire life was a sad failure of nerve, a cruel joke, contrasting bitterly with the swift triumph of this boy whose only merit perhaps was his faith in himself.

He spent a deeply unhappy hour before returning to his mother. He found her talking about domestic matters with Marichette, whom she was helping to put away the beautiful old glass and china into the living-room cupboards.

'Well?' she said, taking Pierre's arm and leading him out into the garden. 'You're on your own?'

'I don't know where they are,' replied Pierre. 'I thought they might have come back here. I walked around the garden but there was no sign of them there. Obviously this long discussion is going to be the final, decisive one.'

'Not necessarily! They may still be looking at the animals! Do go back! Go and find them!'

'I can't let them think I'm watching them and, if they are taking a little romantic stroll in the beech wood, I don't want to draw the servants' attention to Marianne.'

They returned to the living room which Marichette had by now left, and waited there for a quarter of an hour.

Madame André was in a fever of anxiety and vexation. Pierre was silent; he looked heartbroken. At last, Marianne came back alone, a little breathless and smiling.

'Forgive me, my dear friend,' she said, embracing Madame André. 'I am an appalling hostess, but it really is your fault, you should never have brought me such an enterprising young guest.'

'Enterprising!' said Pierre, his tone bitterly ironic.

'Yes, indeed! After all of three hours' acquaintance, he wants me both to fall in love with him and promise to marry him. You must admit, that's rather going it, by any standards.'

'Not if he managed to get you to make up your mind.'

'Oh, my mind is quite made up,' said Marianne.

'So,' said Pierre, in utter dejection, 'I suppose you have come to announce your imminent engagement. Why isn't he with you to proclaim his victory?'

'Rather a modest victory, I'm afraid. He's gone.'

'You mean he's gone back to the house?'

'No, back to Paris.'

'Oh, I see, to get the engagement presents and so forth.'

'I should think he'll soon be buying some, yes, but for some Parisian girl or other,' replied Marianne, 'for he told me he's had enough of country lasses!'

XXII

Madame André jumped up, crying: 'So it's all over between you!'

Marianne looked at Pierre who had been unable to restrain a cry of joy.

'Are you glad?'

'Not if you're sorry.'

'I'm not sorry. All he had in his favour was his nerve, which at first made me think well of him. I thought to myself that with such a self-confident sort of man I shouldn't have to use my own will-power. And I thought that might be very useful. But to be really confident, you have to have good judgement and after a few sentences I could see that although he was very sincere, very witty and very kind, there wasn't a scrap of reason near him. What would I have done, I who am so weak and impressionable, with a brainless husband? It would have been impossible, and since he absolutely insisted on knowing what I thought of him, I told him to his face what I've just said to you.'

'Tell us how it happened,' said Madame André. 'First of all, where were you? Did he propose to you in the cowshed?'

'No, in the meadow, just the other side of that hedge. I'm surprised you didn't hear, we were arguing quite loudly as we walked. As for the declaration, he did it all here, in front of you, with the help of the muscat. There was no need to go into all that again. He brought up the subject of marriage immediately afterwards. Since I'd already made up my mind, I told him straightaway that I didn't want to get married; that's how the argument started. He's not such a nice man when he's crossed. He told me I was a crude little flirt and that I had teased him right through the meal. He said some rather hard things about me and I let him say them because I deserved it. I really had been flirtatious and I'd be lying if I said I hadn't. But it was not for him and since I couldn't confess my secret, I let him think whatever he liked of me.'

'And who was it for?' asked Madame André.

'For someone who will not believe a person loves him unless they tell him so outright. To be that person you need to be at least as bold as Monsieur Philippe. I tried to show it and all I needed was the excitement of his flattery in order to screw up the courage I had always lacked. But my teacher has gone now. I wonder if he really thought me intelligent and pretty. I'm beginning to lose faith in myself already.'

'Marianne! Marianne!' cried Pierre, throwing himself at his god-daughter's knees. 'If you could only understand me, despite all my brutishness! Please forgive me! It's caused me so much suffering already today!'

'And I need your forgiveness for something too,' replied Marianne. 'I'm afraid I read what you wrote in your note-book. You dropped it the day before yesterday in the grass along the little path, while you were telling me about Monsieur Gaucher. I found it on the way home. I thought it was a book of drawings like the ones you often make on your walks. I opened it, I saw my own name and I'm afraid I . . . I'm sorry but I read it all. That evening, I brought the notebook back without saying anything. I put it back on the table in your living room. I knew then that you doubted my love and that you were sorry you could not be the object of it. I wanted to see if you would be jealous of a suitor, if I encouraged him, and now . . .'

'And now,' cried Madame André. 'He is happy! However hard he tried to hide it, I knew all the time how miserable he was and why he was so critical of himself.'

'But I'm not worthy of you, Marianne,' said Pierre, once again overwhelmed. 'I don't deserve you. You are an adorable being and I am . . .'

'Don't say what you think of yourself,' continued Marianne, with emotion. 'You've said enough to me about everything you can think of to discourage me from loving you and you haven't succeeded. This is what's been in my mind for six years. When I thought of you, I couldn't believe you'd be away for so long without coming back. I have been waiting for you always. It's the old peasant patience inculcated in us both since our childhood! When you came back I was a little discouraged, for I could see quite plainly you were determined to stop yourself from loving. Without that notebook I would have thought there was no hope for me. But I took heart again when I read that you were thinking about me despite yourself and then, this morning, when I saw those tears in your eyes . . . We may as well admit it, we love each other. From now on it would be impossible for us to live without each other.'

'Impossible!' replied Pierre. 'There have never been two people so alike as us. The two of us are shy, we sense things keenly, and at the same time, we cannot but be honest and direct with each other. We have the same kinds of feelings, we're each as reluctant as the other to show them in public, yet we yearn to share our delight with each other and to savour each other's company. Our love of the countryside and of nature will no longer be tinged with melancholy as before. What transports of joy to come! What we have both been missing is true, shared love, that boundless confidence and trust in a being other than oneself. At forty, it seems as though my heart has been nourished by dreams alone till now. It is a heart which had never felt true love. Take it! My only present to you! Our past and our future together!'

It was dark when Pierre and his mother left Validat. Madame André felt like walking a little, then climbed into the cart. She let them follow her, for she felt that they must need to speak to each other alone. Marianne walked as far as Dolmor on the arm of her godfather, whom she had begun to call Pierre again, abandoning the formal language forever.

'What a night!' he said to her, as they looked together at the stars. 'What freshness in the air, fragrance in all that surrounds us, the trees, the earth, the very stones themselves! Never were stars so clear as over this fairyland which seems to have grown around us since this morning! Oh if only I had felt this kind of happiness when I was young, then I should have become a great painter or a great poet.'

'Then thank goodness it didn't happen,' replied Marianne. 'For if it had, I should have felt myself so inferior to you, knowing as little as I do about such beautiful things! Sometimes I think I love nature just as much, if not more, for not being able to put it into words. What horrified me about Monsieur Philippe today was the oddly pedantic way he could describe everything he saw. No words can describe some things. The more one says, the less one sees. You see, Pierre, nature is like love, it's in the heart and you mustn't talk about it too much. You diminish what you try to describe. As for myself, I have no idea of my own nature when I act unconsciously. I only see what there is between the sky and myself. I have no part in it at all. If I think of you, in my odd way I *am* you and I cease to exist. That, to me, is real happiness, real poetry, real understanding.'

After Marianne had climbed back into the cart to return and Pierre had entered his own house, he found the following letter left by Philippe:

My dear André,

I have returned to pick up my luggage from your house. I leave with warm thanks for your hospitality. It is through no fault of yours that your pretty little neighbour has made a fool of me. I should have noticed straightaway her clear preference for yourself which, though never admitted, she was never for a moment able to hide. I shall have endured the pangs of unrequited love for the sum total of three or four hours! I shall undoubtedly survive such an ordeal! She is a charming woman and in congratulating you on your happiness, I remain, I hope, both her good friend and your own.

On the following day the banns were announced for the marriage of Pierre André and Marianne Chevreuse.

Bibliography
and Suggestions for Further Reading

Agulhon, Maurice, *Marianne into Battle* (Cambridge University Press, 1981)

Browning, Elizabeth Barrett, *Letters*, 2 vols (London, 1897)

Chomez, Claudine, *George Sand; une étude* (Paris, Seghers, 1973)

Chopin, Frédéric, *Correspondance*, 3 vols (Paris, Richard-Masse, 1953–60)

Dolléans, Edouard, *Féminisme et mouvement ouvrier*: (Paris, Les Editions ouvrières, 1951)

Dostoevsky, Fyodor, *Journal d'un ecrivain* (Paris, Charpentier, 1904)

Dunilac, Julien, *George Sand sous la loupe* (Genève, Slatkine, Paris, Champion, 1978)

Goncourt, Edmond et Jules de, *Journal*, 3 vols (Paris, 1888)

Jacobs, Alphonse, Gustave Flaubert-George Sand *Correspondance* (Paris, Flammarion, 1981)

James, Henry, *French Poets and Novelists* (London, 1884)

Jordan, Ruth, *George Sand: a Biography* (Constable, 1976)

Karenine, Wladimir, *George Sand: sa vie et ses oeuvres*, 4 vols (Paris, Ollendorf, Plon-Nourrit, 1899–1926)

Mallet, Francine, *George Sand* (Paris, Grasset, 1976)

Marix-Spire, Thérèse, *Les Romantiques et la musique: le cas George Sand* (Nouvelles Editions Latines, 1954)

Musset, Alfred de, *Correspondance 1827–57* (Paris, 1907)

Pailleron, Marie-Louise, *George Sand et les hommes de '48* (Grasset, 1953)

Starkie, Enid, *Flaubert – The Making of the Master* (London, 1967)

Steegmuller, Francis, *The Letters of Gustave Flaubert*, 2 vols (London, Faber & Faber, 1984)

Thomson, Patricia, *George Sand and the Victorians* (Macmillan, 1977)

Tricotel, Claude, *Comme deux troubadours: Histoire de l'amitié Flaubert-Sand* (Societé d'édition d'enseignement supérieur, 1978)

Vincent, Marie-Louise, *George Sand et le Berry* (Genève, Slatkine Reprints, 1978)

Winwar, Frances, *The Life of the Heart: George Sand and her Times* (Harper & Row, 1945)

Zeldin, Theodore, *France 1848–1945, Volume 1: Ambition and Love* (Oxford University Press, 1979)

Chronology of Selected Works